*Great news! From this month onward,
Harlequin Presents® is offering you more!*

Now, when you go to your local bookstore, you'll
find that you have *eight* Harlequin Presents® titles
to choose from—more of your favorite authors,
more of the stories you love.

To help you make your selection from our July
books, here are the fabulous titles that are available:
Prince of the Desert by Penny Jordan—hot desert
nights! *The Scorsolini Marriage Bargain* by
Lucy Monroe—the final part of an unforgettable
royal trilogy! *Naked in His Arms* by Sandra Marton—
the third Knight Brothers story and a sensationally
sensual read to boot! *The Secret Baby Revenge* by
Emma Darcy—a passionate Latin lover and a shocking
secret from his past! *At the Greek Tycoon's Bidding*
by Cathy Williams—an ordinary girl and the most
gorgeous Greek millionaire! *The Italian's Convenient
Wife* by Catherine Spencer—passion, tears and joy
as a marriage is announced! *The Jet-Set Seduction*
by Sandra Field—fasten your seat belt and prepare
to be whisked away to glamorous foreign locations!
Mistress on Demand by Maggie Cox—he's rich,
ruthless and really...irresistible!

Remember, in July, Harlequin Presents® promises
more reading pleasure. Enjoy!

Royal Brides

The Scorsolini Princes:

Proud rulers and passionate lovers
who need convenient wives!

*Welcome to this brand-new miniseries set in
glamorous and exotic places known as the
USIC (United Small Independent Countries)—
it's a world filled with passion, romance
and royals!*

Don't miss this new trilogy by Lucy Monroe

The Prince's Virgin Wife—May
His Royal Love-Child—June
The Scorsolini Marriage Bargain—July

Lucy Monroe

THE SCORSOLINI MARRIAGE BARGAIN

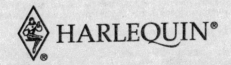

TORONTO • NEW YORK • LONDON
AMSTERDAM • PARIS • SYDNEY • HAMBURG
STOCKHOLM • ATHENS • TOKYO • MILAN • MADRID
PRAGUE • WARSAW • BUDAPEST • AUCKLAND

ISBN-13: 978-0-373-12548-7
ISBN-10:   0-373-12548-8

THE SCORSOLINI MARRIAGE BARGAIN

First North American Publication 2006.

All about the author...
Lucy Monroe

LUCY MONROE sold her first book in September 2002 to the Harlequin Presents line. That book represented a dream that had been burning in her heart for years...the dream to share her stories with readers who love romance as much as she does. Since then she has sold more than thirty books to three publishers and hit national bestsellers lists in the U.S. and England, but what has touched her most deeply since selling that first book are the reader letters she receives. Her most important goal with every book is to touch a reader's heart and it is this connection that makes those nights spent writing into the wee hours worth it.

She started reading Harlequin Presents books very young and discovered a heroic type of man between the covers of those books...an honorable man, capable of faithfulness and sacrifice for the people he loves. Now married to what she terms her "alpha male at the end of a book," Lucy believes there is a lot more reality to the fantasy stories she writes than most people give credit for. She believes happy endings are really marvelous beginnings and that's why she writes them. She hopes her books help readers to believe a little, too...just like romance did for her so many years ago.

Lucy enjoys hearing from readers and responds to every e-mail. You can reach her by e-mailing lucymonroe@lucymonroe.com.

For Marilyn Shoemaker, a dear friend and valued reader. Your support and encouragement means the world! And thank you for helping me to name the secondary islands Diamante, Rubino & Zaffiro, of Isole dei Re for this trilogy.

Hugs,
Lucy

CHAPTER ONE

"SOME days, being a princess is right up there with long-term incarceration on Alcatraz." Therese muttered the words as she pulled up the zip on her favorite mint-green sheath dress while preparing for yet another formal dinner in the Palazzo di Scorsolini.

It wasn't the prospect of one more dinner eaten with King Vincente and the dignitaries who had come to visit him that made her cranky, though. It was frustration with a day spent in her own version of purgatory. She loved the king of Isole dei Re and was closer to him than her own father.

But there were still times she wished she and Claudio had their own home, not just a set of apartments in the royal palace of Lo Paradiso. No matter how beautiful, the suite afforded little privacy when she and Claudio were expected to eat most meals in the formal dining room. The fact that her duties as princess ruled even her personal time could be a major drawback. Especially tonight, when she was jittery with the need to share the news she'd received from her doctor in Miami. She'd gone to the States for this particular examination in order to guarantee absolute discretion.

She almost wished she hadn't now. Because if the press

had gotten hold of the story, at least she would be saved from having to impart the news to Claudio.

It was a craven thought and she was no coward.

But even she, with years of training as a diplomat's daughter, could not look on the end of her marriage with equanimity. Unlike her parents, she did not see life as a series of political and social moves and countermoves. For her…real life hurt.

Claudio finished putting on his second cuff link and pulled both sleeves straight with precise, familiar movements that made her heart ache at the prospect of losing that familiarity. His lips twisted, giving his gorgeous face a cynical cast. "I will be sure and tell your mother you think so."

Therese stopped on her way to the table where she had left the jewelry she planned to wear tonight. "Don't you dare."

Claudio found her mother's social climbing tendencies a source of amusement, but Therese was not so sanguine. She, after all, was the ladder her mother expected to climb up on.

"I have no desire to listen to Lecture 101 from Mother on how lucky I am to be a princess, or how privileged my life is." Not to mention the bit about how amazing it was that Claudio had chosen Therese from amongst all of the eligible women in the world. She really didn't want to hear that particular treatise, right now.

"Perhaps she will be able to understand your apparent disenchantment with your lot in life better than I can." The edge in Claudio's voice said he was only partially kidding and his dark gaze was serious and probing.

"I'm not disenchanted with my lot." Merely devastated by it, but now was not the time to tell him so.

And she couldn't help feeling her charmed life had been cursed…probably from the beginning, but she'd been too blind to see it. She'd bought into the fairy tale only to discover that love on one side brought pain, not pleasure. The happily-ever-after was only for princesses in storybook land…or those who were loved for themselves, like the two women married to the other Scorsolini princes.

"Then what is this comparing being my wife to that of a convict incarcerated in prison?" Claudio towered over her with his six-foot-four-inch frame, his scent surrounding her and reminding her just how much she would miss the physical reality of his presence when it was gone.

He was every woman's dream, the kind of prince that fairy tales really were made of. She had woven enough fantasies around him to know. He had black hair, rich brown eyes and the dark skin tone of his Sicilian forefathers, but the height of a professional athlete. His body was muscular, without an ounce of fat anywhere and his face could have been that of an American film star…perhaps of a different era, though. No pretty boy looks, but rugged angles and a cleft chin that bespoke a strength of character that she had come to rely on completely.

She had to swallow twice before speaking. "I did not say being *your wife* was like that."

"You said *the life of a princess,* which you would not be if you were not married to me."

"True." She sighed. "But I didn't mean to offend you."

He cupped her cheek in a move guaranteed to send her nerve endings rioting. He so rarely touched her when they were not in bed that when he did so, she didn't know how to handle it.

"I am not offended, merely concerned." She could hear that concern in his voice and it made her feel guilty.

He had done nothing wrong…except choose the incorrect woman to be his princess. "It has been a rough day, that's all."

His second hand joined the first and he tilted her face up so she could not hope to avoid his discerning gaze. "Why?"

She licked her lips, wishing again they were not going downstairs for dinner with his father. She wished even more that the twinges of pain in her pelvis were just the regular preperiod cramps she had believed them to be when she first went off the pill so they could try for a baby. "I spent the whole morning with representatives of Isole dei Re's foremost women's organization discussing the need for day care services and preschools on the islands."

He frowned as if he couldn't understand what bothered her about that. She'd had many such meetings and they had all gone rather well. However, all he said was, "I thought Tomasso's wife was spearheading that."

"The helicopter flight between the islands exacerbates Maggie's morning sickness, but she didn't want to put the meeting off. I convinced her to let me take her place. Looking back, I should have had the delegates flown to Diamante to meet with her instead."

His hands dropped from her face and she felt an immediate chill from the withdrawal, though she was sure he hadn't meant it that way. "Why? You and Maggie share views on this subject. You have certainly discussed it enough to cover all the points adequately."

"Not according to the delegates." She grimaced. "They felt that a woman without children, moreover one who had never been forced to work for her living, could not comprehend the challenges faced by working mothers. They believe that Maggie is ideal for this endeavor and that I should keep right out of it."

"They said this to you?" He didn't sound offended on her behalf, merely curious. He could have no idea how much the other women's disapproval had hurt.

She felt both exhausted and savaged, especially after the phone call from her doctor in Miami. "Yes."

"It is a good thing that you grew up learning political diplomacy then."

"Meaning it might have upset you if I had told them all to take a flying leap?"

Claudio gave a masculine chuckle as if he could not imagine such a thing. "As if you would."

"Maybe I did."

But he just shook his head. "I know you. No chance."

"Maybe you don't know me as well as you think you do." In fact, she knew he didn't. After all, he'd never once latched on to the fact that she'd married him because she loved him. The marriage of convenience aspect had been a plan hatched in his and her mother's more mercenary brains.

"Did you?" he asked with a sardonic brow raised.

She wanted to say yes just to prove him wrong, but told the truth instead. "No, but *I wanted to.*"

"What we want and what we allow ourselves to do are rarely the same thing. And it is a testament to your suitability to your position that you live by this stricture."

She turned away from him and started putting on her jewelry. "And you wonder why I compared being a princess to being a prisoner?"

"Are you unhappy, Therese?"

"No more than most people," she admitted. She'd been raised from the time she was a tiny child to hide her true emotion, but she was so tired of pretending.

"You are unhappy?" Claudio demanded in a voice laced with unmistakable shock.

The man so well-known in diplomatic circles for his perspicacity was thick as a brick where she was concerned.

"Two of the delegates were less than subtle in expressing their belief it was past time I gave you an heir," she said instead of answering.

"And this upset you?" Again the shocked surprise.

"A little."

"But it should not. Soon you will be able to share happy news on that score."

She winced as his words sprinkled salt into wounds left open and bleeding by the doctor's phone call.

"And if I can't?" she asked, testing waters she was not ready to tread into.

His big, warm hands landed on her shoulders and he turned her to face him with inexorable movements. "You are bothered that you have not yet conceived? You should not be. We have only been trying for a few months. The doctor said that women who have been on the pill for a prolonged time can take longer to get pregnant, but it will happen soon enough. After all, we know everything is in working order."

Worse than salt on wounds, those words were like the lashing of a cruelly wielded whip. Prior to marrying three years ago, he had required they go through several tests including blood type and the compatibility of his sperm with the mucus on her cervix. He had also requested she have her fertility cycles tested, just to be sure.

Knowing that a big part of why he was marrying her was so that she could provide heirs for the Scorsolini throne, she had agreed without argument. Everything had come back normal. They were compatible for pregnancy and she was as fertile as any other woman her age.

The biggest surprise for her had been his desire to wait to have children for a while. She hadn't understood it, still wasn't sure why he had requested they wait, but now she knew that whatever chance they had of making babies together was over.

Unable to stand any level of intimacy in the face of what she knew was to come, even such a simple touch, she turned away from him.

Helpless anger filled Claudio as Therese moved from him, her womanly curves taunting a libido that ached for her night and day. He wanted to grab her back and demand to know why after three years his touch was no longer acceptable, but that would be the act of a primitive man and the crown prince of Isole dei Re was in no way primitive.

Besides, physical rejection from her was not a new thing. It had been happening for months now, but each time she turned away from a physical connection, it still shocked him. After two years of receiving an incredibly passionate response on every occasion when he touched her, he could be forgiven for finding it nearly impossible to reconcile to her sudden change of heart.

Prior to the last few months, he would have sworn that Therese loved him. She'd never said so, but for the first two years of their marriage, she had shown in many subtle and not so subtle ways that she felt more for him than the mercenary satisfaction of a woman for a marriage well contracted. Her love had not been one of his requirements, so he had not dwelt on it too much…until it was gone.

It was not that he needed the emotion from her, but he could not help wondering where it had gone and why she no longer seemed to want him with the latent passion that had drawn him to her in the first place.

Her physical rejections had started a month or so after she went off the pill so they could try for a baby. At first, he had thought that maybe her hormones had been at fault. After all, he'd read about that sort of thing happening, but in the intervening months it had gotten worse, not better.

Then sometimes she would make love with him the way she used to and all his concerns on that score would disappear. Only to reappear when she turned him down again. He was not a man who had suffered much rejection in his life, particularly from a woman he desired physically. For it to come from his own wife was totally unacceptable.

And it had been happening more and more lately.

He'd begun to wonder if deep down, she did not want to get pregnant. "Do you not want my baby? Are you frightened of what will happen?"

She flinched as if he'd slapped her, her face going unnaturally pale. "Yes, I want your baby. *More than anything*. I don't know how you could believe anything else."

She was so fervent he could not doubt her. "Then there is nothing about this situation that should upset you."

The look she gave him from her green eyes was not encouraging, but he forged on, certain of his own conclusions. "Soon enough you will be able to silence busybodies with the reality of a pregnancy. As for today, you will simply play the scenario differently next time and send the delegates to meet with Maggie."

She spun to face the mirror and pulled her silky, long brown hair up into a twist on the back of her head with deft fingers, securing it with a clip. "And that makes it all okay, does it?"

"It should," he said with some exasperation. "I do not understand why you are reacting so strongly to this. You have dealt with far more annoying people than these women."

Therese shrugged her delicate shoulders and headed toward the door. She was so beautiful, almost ethereal in her appearance despite curves that proclaimed her one hundred percent woman. And times like this he felt as if she was as untouchable as a spirit. But she was his wife, it was his right to touch her.

He did it, taking her arm as she walked by.

She stopped and looked up at him, her beautiful green gaze filled with a vulnerability he did not understand and liked even less. It implied an unhappiness he did not want her to feel.

"What?" she demanded.

"I do not like to see you like this."

"I know. You expect everything in your life to go smoothly, every person to fulfill their role without question. Your schedule is regimented to the nth degree and surprises are few and far between."

"I take great pains to make it so."

"Even to the point of marrying a woman with all the proper qualifications. You had me investigated, tested and then tested me yourself to be sure of my fit as your *principessa* and future queen. I am certain you never expected me to be a source of frustration for you."

She was right, but he didn't understand the bitter undertone in her voice. She had not seemed to mind his endeavors to make sure of her suitability at the time. "You are everything I wanted in a wife. Naturally in my position, I would make every effort to make certain our future was assured, but you were and are perfect for me, *cara*."

She flinched at the endearment, much as she frequently flinched from his touch anymore. As if any allusion to intimacy between the two of them hurt her. But they were intimate. They were husband and wife. There was no relationship more intimate than that.

So why did he feel like they existed in completely different hemispheres at the moment?

He pulled her close, ignoring the subtle stiffening of her body. "We do not have to go down to dinner, you know."

Her eyes widened in surprise. "Your father is entertaining dignitaries from Venezuela."

"They are his fishing buddies."

"They are official diplomats."

"He will not care if we send word we are not coming. And there are far more interesting ways for us to spend the evening than listening to fishing stories."

"Talking?"

"That is not what I had in mind."

Her face set, she pulled away, her rejection as obvious as it was final. "That would be rude."

Had Therese found someone else who engaged her affectionate nature? Perhaps she had even taken a lover. Rage poured through him at the thought, but in his arrogance he could think of nothing else that would explain the way she rejected him physically. Add that to the fact that at times she acted like her mind was definitely not in the here and now, and he had a compelling argument for believing she had found someone else.

So compelling he was not sure he could control the fury his reasoning evoked. He hated feeling like that. He had married her in order to avoid this kind of emotional upheaval in his life.

Which was the primary reason he had never voiced his suspicion. He knew Therese better than most men knew their wives. He's made sure of it and everything he knew of her character said she would never, under any circumstances act so dishonorably as to have an affair. That was one of the reasons he had married her. She was a woman of fierce integrity, but she had also used to be a woman of intense passions.

If the one could change…could the other? Did some unknown man have claim on her secret sensuality that used to delight Claudio so much? He could not believe it of her, but as unlikely as it might seem, he had to know the truth.

He would call the detective agency Tomasso had used to trace and investigate Maggie and order an investigation of Therese's present activities and past movements for the last year. Hawke, the owner of the international detective agency, was wholly discreet and the very best at what he did.

One way, or another, Claudio was going to get to the bottom of the mystery of his wife's behavior. If another man was involved, he would find out and deal with the situation accordingly.

The thought brought a surge of primitive anger he had no intention of giving in to.

Therese regretted rejecting Claudio's invitation throughout dinner. So what if all he wanted was sex? She could have made him listen. The problem was, she didn't want to. As long as she kept the news to herself, part of her could go on pretending her marriage had a chance. But even if they had talked…even if they'd made love and it had hurt a little, she would have one more memory stored up for a future without him. Instead she was sitting with a smile pasted on her face while conversation she had no interest in flowed around her. Claudio had been right. King Vincente and his fishing buddies from Venezuela were too busy swapping stories to even notice her and Claudio's presence at the table.

Claudio had gotten a phone call halfway through dinner and disappeared to answer it, leaving her entirely to her own devices. Not that he'd been all that communicative beforehand. He was too much the crown prince to make his displeasure with her obvious to the others at the table, but she had felt it.

Just as she had known he would not come back once he had left to take the phone call. He had often chosen work over her company. Tonight would certainly be no different. So, when it came time to take their coffee in the other room, she excused herself.

She'd been feeling twinges of pain in her pelvic area all day even though her menses were not due for a few days. Every month the pain got worse and it no longer limited itself to the days of her monthly. According to her doctor, that was typical for her condition, but it certainly wasn't pleasant.

It was getting harder and harder to hide the truth from Claudio as well, but soon…she wouldn't have to. She would tell him the results of the laparoscopy she'd had performed in secret on a trip to Miami. Then she would tell him what the doctor had said her condition meant for the future and he would tell her that their marriage was over.

The thought was far worse than the pain in her lower abdomen and she forced her mind to deal with the present, not the probable future.

Maybe a long, hot soak coupled with a couple of over the counter pain meds would suffice and she wouldn't be forced to take one of the pain-killing bombs the doctor had prescribed.

They always left her feeling so loopy and she hated it. There were days she couldn't even remember what she'd done because she'd spent so much of her time in a fog. The shock was that Claudio had never noticed. If she needed proof that she was nothing more to him than a convenience, that was it.

How could a man, even a man as oblivious to the normal issues of life as Claudio, not notice his wife had the behavior pattern of a drug addict? But he never said anything when she was zoned out on pain meds. To give him credit, she did her best to hide her condition from him…in every way. But there was a big part of her that resented the fact it was so easy.

If he cared at all, it wouldn't be. She was sure of it.

Her heart heavy, she started a bath. No woman should have to live with the constant knowledge that she loved where there was no reciprocating emotion to be had. It hurt too much.

Once the bath was full, she dimmed the lights in the en suite and poured soothing aromatherapy oil into the steaming water. Then, while the whirlpool jets mixed the water, sending forth a soft fragrance, she took her pain meds. She shed her robe, letting the silk fall to the floor and not caring that she should have hung it up. Refusing to even think about how the responsible Therese would have taken care of it so someone else would not have to, the in-pain-and-tired-of-hiding-it Therese slid into bathtub.

She'd been soaking for thirty minutes when she heard sounds in the bedroom. She'd let her mind float, so it only registered on the periphery of her consciousnesses what those sounds meant.

"If you've fallen asleep in there, I'm going to be more than mildly annoyed with you."

Her eyes slid open and the impact of his presence slammed into her like it always did. No man should be this beautiful. "Not sleeping. No need to be irritated."

"You certainly looked asleep," he said accusingly, but his dark eyes were eating her up in a way that said bathtub safety was not the only thing on his mind.

His obvious interest found an answering hunger in her body. The effectiveness of the hot bath and painkillers meant she could act on it if she wanted to and she did. Once she told him the truth and he accepted there was only one practical solution for their future, she would have to live the rest of her life without feeling the things his touch invoked.

"I don't suppose you would consider being my bathtub buddy?" she asked, giving his magnificent body a once-over. "Purely for safety's sake, you understand."

His eyes narrowed. "Is that an invitation?"

"What do you think?"

"I think I don't understand why you forced me to sit through an hour of fishing stories if you were feeling like this." He made a sound that was suspiciously like a growl of frustration, while his lower body reacted in a basic and obvious way to her suggestion.

She hid her smile of satisfaction at the evidence that if nothing else, the man wanted her. Then she looked up at him from between her lashes. "Are you saying you're not interested?" she asked in a tone that said she didn't believe it. "Your body says otherwise."

"Maybe my body isn't the one in control here."

She arched her back, relief coursing through her when the

shift in her pelvis the movement caused didn't so much as result in a tiny twinge of discomfort. "Maybe it should be."

"Damn it, Therese, what is going on?"

He never swore in front of her. It shocked her so much that she relaxed back into the water. What if he *didn't* want her? A man might not be able to control the physical responses of his body, but he didn't have to give in to them. Not if his mind was turned off in spite of his body's cravings.

He was upset with her for turning him down earlier. She should have realized he would be, but normally he acted as if her diminished desire didn't impact him at all. After all, he was a busy man. He had about as much time for sex as he did for meaningful conversations with her, which meant he had almost no time at all.

Saying nothing because she was afraid she'd beg if she did, she stood to get out of the tub.

"What are you doing?" he asked in a low growl.

"What does it look like? I'm getting out." He could turn her down, but he didn't need to rub her nose in it.

He made a sound that sent a shiver down her spine. "Stay where you are, you provoking little witch."

CHAPTER TWO

"I WASN'T trying to provoke you," she denied.

He yanked his tie off and started on the buttons of his shirt. "Then I don't want to see what you are like when you do try."

It suddenly occurred to her that he *wasn't* turning her down, but intended to get into the oversize tub with her. She smiled in pure relief. "Are you sure about that?"

He jerked his pants down, pulling his shorts with them and revealing the impressive length of his angrily throbbing erection. He *really* wanted her, but from the expression on his face, he wasn't happy about it.

He stepped into the tub and pulled her to him all in one movement, rubbing his rigid length against her in a blatantly sexual gesture. "I'm not sure about much of anything with you anymore."

She wrapped her arms around his neck, reveling in the feel of his hard muscles and heated skin against her. "I thought you were always sure of me…about everything."

"I wish." His mouth slammed down onto hers and there was none of the seductive finesse she'd come to expect from him.

Something had really upset him and he was barely in control. Her ultraurbane husband was showing a basic side to his nature he'd always kept carefully hidden. She doubted he even knew it was there. She had always suspected, though. She saw glimpses sometimes when they were making love, but this was the first time she sensed his control was really at risk. She didn't mind. In fact, she loved it.

Uncomplicated passion was exactly what she needed right now to get her mind off things she could not stand to think about. She kissed him back, letting the desperation she felt translate into a physical need that more than matched his. A growl rumbled low in his chest and he deepened the kiss with a thrust of his tongue that took total possession of her mouth.

She let her fingers run down the hard contours of his chest, tangling in his black, curling hair and tugging gently.

His mouth broke from hers. "*Sì, cara.* You know how much I like that. Do it again."

She did and then bent forward to taste the salt of his skin with the tip of her tongue. If only he could love her and not merely what she could do to him. But thinking along those lines would bring pain, not pleasure and she slammed the door shut on that part of her mind with a ferocious clang.

She nuzzled him, loving his scent and the feel of his warmth against her face. He was so perfect for her physically.

His big hands cupped her bottom and he lifted, rubbing his erection against the juncture of her thighs bringing forth a damp throb of response that she wallowed in. She made a mewling sound, her need so intense she dug her fingers like claws into his hot skin.

She loved him so much and in this—for right now, he was absolutely and totally hers.

She pressed her breasts against his chest and rubbed side

to side, the stimulation to her aching peaks along with the way he was bringing their bodies together intimately almost enough to send her over the edge.

Suddenly he dropped into the water with her on top of him, sending hot, scented waves sloshing over the sides of the tub and onto the marble floor. He spread her legs so she straddled him and thrust upward pulling her down with a near-bruising grip on her hips. His aim was perfect and his rigid length speared into her, filling her completely in one powerful thrust.

Her body jerked at the shocking intrusion, but it didn't even sort of hurt.

It felt so good, so right…so tight. They fit each other so absolutely perfectly in this way…how could her body make her imperfect for him in the one way that mattered most?

His mouth tore from hers. "What is it? What's the matter?"

She stared at him, her eyes burning with tears she would never let him see. "Nothing. You feel so incredible inside me," she panted.

"You went stiff."

"It's always a little tight at first."

He smiled, masculine ego glowing from his dark eyes. "Yes, but you like it, no?"

"I love it." *I love you,* she whispered deep in her heart. *Forever.*

"Then let me take you again."

"Yes."

And she did, thrilled by the lack of pain and hoping it would last the entire lovemaking session. She was careful not to take him too deep and he let her control things. She'd often teased him this way in the past and it was highly pleasurable for both of them.

Putting his head back and breathing harshly, his face contorted with pleasure, he said, "You are so good at this."

"And you are incredible."

He went stiff beneath her, his body filled with a tension that had nothing to do with sensual delight. "Then why do you turn me down so often lately?" he asked, his voice edged with dark emotion.

She didn't have an answer...at least not one she was prepared to discuss right now when the pleasure was on the verge of letting her forget everything. So, instead of saying something that might mess that up, she kissed him.

He kissed her back, his mouth quickly taking control and then claiming her lips as if intent on punishment. Only she didn't feel punished. She responded with ferocity of her own and increased the pace of their lovemaking until she felt the pleasure spiral tight inside her and she went through the stratosphere, all rational thought flying from her mind as her body convulsed with the ultimate satisfaction.

He grabbed her hips and thrust upward, once, twice... three times and sent her into a second climax, so close to the first that her lungs seized along with everything else.

He shouted and she felt his warmth inside of her as she took a long shuddering breath into her oxygen-starved lungs before collapsing on top of him.

She kissed his chest. "That was wonderful."

"Yes," he said, his breathing still heavy. "It always is."

"Yes."

"So, why—"

She put her hand over his mouth. "No talking. Just enjoy. Okay?"

He frowned.

"Please," she pleaded.

He nodded, one quick jerk of his head.

She smiled and let her head settle against his chest again. "I wish we could stay like this forever."

"You said no talking."

"So I did." She kissed him again because she couldn't help herself and then relaxed there.

His hands moved from her hips to her back and she cuddled in the circle of his arms, their bodies still connected in the most intimate way possible.

Eventually he carried her to the oversize glass shower stall and they made love again under the cascading spray before washing and then going to bed where she fell asleep as soon as her head hit the pillow.

She woke up alone and buried her face in his pillow, wallowing in Claudio's lingering scent.

The night before had been incredible. He'd woken her sometime in the early hours of the morning and made love to her with such tender gentleness, she had cried when she climaxed. He'd held her afterward, rubbing her back and whispering how much he enjoyed her body and how beautiful she was in Italian.

But after three years, she realized being beautiful to him was not enough. It was not love and could not last forever because outer beauty did not last forever. And outstanding sexual satisfaction could not make up for her inability to give him the one thing he expected from her.

Heirs for the Scorsolini throne.

It was time to tell him the truth.

But when she went downstairs, it was to discover he'd flown out for a meeting in New York. She'd forgotten all about his trip and didn't know if she could wait the three days until his return to settle things between them.

She didn't miss the fact that he'd left without bothering to wake her and kiss her goodbye, either. Somehow, that made everything worse. Maybe because it was a huge indication of the lack of true intimacy in their relationship and any real reliance he had on her.

There wasn't any. They were married, but she was no more necessary to his life than any of his other many employees. If it wasn't for the sex, their relationship would not be any more personal than it was with any of the others, either. And when the sex wasn't on, neither was their relationship. How many business trips had he scheduled during her monthly? Had he ever once asked her to accompany him? No.

She was a convenience to him and she might as well admit it.

But damn it, it hurt.

She needed to be more to him. The only hope for their future was for her to mean something more to him. Which meant there was no hope at all.

Her mobile phone chirped and she scooted up in bed to answer it. When she saw that it was Claudio, her breath caught. She flipped it open. "Hello?"

"Good morning, *bella*."

For some reason that endearment hurt this morning. Wasn't she more than a face and a body to him? Was her value truly determined by her outer looks and her poise as her mother had always insisted it was?

"Good morning, Claudio." She waited expectantly for him to get to the purpose of his phone call.

"I'm on my way to my hotel and wishing you were with me."

Her heart stopped. "Are you really?"

"*Sì*. I do not like when our schedules separate us."

"Then why didn't you ask me to come with you?" she asked, hope uncurling like a slow bud inside her heart.

"You have your obligations. I have mine."

"And do the obligations always come first?"

"They must. It is our duty."

"They don't always for Tomasso and Maggie or Marcello and Danette." But then his brothers were in love with their wives.

One of the things that had hurt the most this past few months was seeing what a Scorsolini prince in love acted like and acknowledging it was nothing like Claudio's behavior toward her.

"My brothers are not in line to be the next ruler of Isole dei Re. They can afford to put duty second on occasion. The country does not depend so heavily on them. And their wives do not have the same requirements put upon you as my wife." He spoke like a teacher reciting a lesson to a student that he had recited many times before.

The practiced patience in his voice was worse than if he'd snapped at her.

"I miss you," she said baldly.

"I have been gone less than a day."

"Are you saying you don't miss me?" she asked, wishing the question did not feel like a razor shredding her insides. So much for him wishing she was there.

"I will miss you tonight."

If he had planned it, he could not have said anything more wounding. "In bed," she said flatly.

"We are good there."

"But nowhere else?" she asked, for once making no effort to hide how much that displeased her.

"Do not be ridiculous. You are my wife, not my concubine. Why would you even ask such a question?"

"Perhaps because that is the only place you deign to miss me."

"I did not say that."

"Excuse me, but you did."

"I did not call you to get into an argument." The frozen tone of his voice came across the phone line loud and clear. "But for the record, if you took what I said to mean such a thing, it did not."

Maybe he didn't know he meant it that way, but he had. The facts spoke for themselves.

"Why *did* you call? We both know it was not merely to say hello. I don't rate those kinds of phone calls from you."

"What is the matter with you? Perhaps that is *exactly* why I called."

She wasn't even remotely convinced. "Not likely."

"I was thinking of you and wanted to hear your voice, all right?" he asked, sounding thoroughly annoyed with her.

Oh. Man. Did he mean it?

Of course he meant it. Claudio never consciously lied, but still she had to ask, "Is that true?"

"I do not make it a habit of lying to you."

"I know you don't. It's one of the things I appreciate most about you."

Her father had lied to her, to her mother, to anyone at all…all for the sake of convenience and had called it diplomacy. But she didn't think that that kind of diplomacy belonged in a family. It was best saved for other politicians, all of whom were expecting it.

"Can you say the same thing?"

Shock coursed through her that he would ask such a thing. "Of course I can. You know I don't lie to you."

"Only perhaps you do not feel withholding information from me is the same as lying?" he asked.

Could he know about her condition? Impossible…she'd been far too careful to keep it a secret. "I don't know what you mean." That at least was no lie, but it was also not the full truth. Perhaps there was more of her father in her than she wanted to admit.

"Are you sure about that?"

"No one tells everything, but that doesn't mean I lie to you," she said, defending a position he did not know why she'd taken. But there was no way she could tell him the news of her infertility over the phone.

"I hope that is true, Therese." He sighed. "I have another call coming in. I have to go."

"All right. Goodbye, Claudio."

"Goodbye, *bella*."

She hung up the phone, but as she got ready for the day and then left her apartments to traverse the grand marbled hallways of the palace, she couldn't stop thinking about what he had said, what she had said and what she hadn't been able to say. She owed him the truth—both about her condition and what she planned to do because of it.

He would be relieved. He had to be.

But a tiny part of her heart hoped against all logic that he wouldn't be. That he might even refuse to let her do the right thing…the only logical thing to do in the circumstances.

Walk away.

"Your Highness…"

Therese looked up from her musings to find her personal

secretary standing in front of her. At one time Ida had worked for her mother, but the year Therese had married, her mom had sacked Ida in order to hire someone else. The other woman was younger and had connections high in the social set Therese's parents were now moving in. Ida had been only too happy to accept Therese's offer of a job.

Ida's loyalty was unwavering, her discretion without equal and her finesse with a schedule second to none. She was the only other person besides Therese's Miami doctor and his assistant who knew about the laparoscopy and the results.

"Your morning appointment is waiting."

"Ida…I have to go to New York."

The older woman barely blinked. "I believe I can clear your schedule. If you could take care of your current appointment, I will have a maid pack for you while I begin clearing your schedule."

"Just like that?"

"There are things you and the prince need to talk about," Ida said kindly. "I'm assuming those things did not get said last night."

Therese shook her head.

"That gives a trip to New York precedence over anything else in your schedule."

"I hope Claudio feels that way."

"Men, even brilliant men, are not always the brightest spark when it comes to relationships."

"Even brilliant men, hmm?"

"Yes." Ida sighed, the sound filled with exasperation. "Sometimes I think it's the really bright ones that are dumbest when it comes to women."

Therese laughed. She thought maybe Ida was right. Look at how stupid King Vincente was about Flavia.

"Just you remember, young lady…a marriage is not all about having children."

Therese smiled disappeared. "My marriage is."

"Don't you believe it."

She wished she shared the older woman's assurance, but she couldn't.

She landed in New York later that evening, her nerves stretched to screaming point. She'd spent the entire flight going over in her head what she was going to say to Claudio, but she couldn't get past the first sally because every time she thought about him agreeing that their marriage should be dissolved, her throat clogged with tears.

She had asked security not to alert her husband to her intention to join him. For some reason, she felt the element of surprise might be on her side. She was informed he was at the hotel preparing for a dinner meeting when her plane landed. It seemed fortuitous and she hoped it boded well for the meeting to come.

Her eyes barely registered the opulence of the oversize suite when security let her inside. She was too busy trying to control her tortured emotions.

Claudio was tying his tie when she walked into the bedroom.

"Hello, *caro*."

His big body jerked, blatant testament to how shocked he was by her presence. Then his head snapped up, his dark eyes zeroing in on her with physical intensity. "*Therese*, what are you doing here?"

"You said you'd like it if I was."

"You are not here because of my phone call this morning." His expression dared her to contradict him…to lie.

"No, I'm not. We need to talk."

"Do we?"

"Yes," she said, trying to ignore the fact that his expression was about as welcoming as an accountant faced with a tax auditor.

"I suppose you have something you have to confess that has weighed on your conscience long enough," he said in a voice that dripped in ice.

She didn't know what triggered his hostility, except maybe that she'd changed her schedule. Claudio didn't like surprises and he had a worse one coming.

"You could put it that way." She couldn't even assure him it was nothing bad because it was.

In a marriage like theirs, it was a death knell and nothing less.

Claudio went back to what he was doing with cold precision. "It will have to wait. I have a dinner meeting."

"Can you cancel it?"

"You mean like you obviously canceled all of your obligations so you could fly up here and have a conversation that surely could have waited the three days it would take me to get home?"

"Yes." She didn't care how he made it sound. That was exactly what she wanted.

"That's not going to happen."

"Would it really be so terrible?"

"Obviously you do not consider it so, but I do not appreciate my wife letting down her obligations and therefore me."

"And are our duties the only thing that matter in our life together?"

"Duty must come first. At one time, I believe you understood this."

"Is that why you married me?"

"You already know it was one of the primary reasons I decided you would suit me well as a wife. Your parents could not have raised you more suitably for the life of a princess if they had been royalty themselves."

That reminder was as unwelcome as it was painful. For she better than anyone knew how carefully her parents had raised her. Her father with the hopes she would pursue a political career and her mother with the desire to live her life's ambitions through her daughter. Neither had ever cared what dreams beat in Therese's heart.

"My appreciation for duty was my main attraction to you...and of course the fact that I was physically compatible with you," she said, long denied hurt coming out as bitterness.

"Would you have expected me to marry a woman who did not understand or fit the role of princess and future queen?"

"Your brothers weren't so worried about suitability when they chose their wives," she reminded him.

"As I said last night, I am not my brothers."

"No, you are the crown prince, which means duty must come first, last and always with you."

"You knew this when we married. It is not something I expect to be raised as an issue of contention now."

"You don't expect anything to be raised as an issue of contention."

"How perceptive of you to realize that." He pulled on his black dinner jacket. "As scintillating as this conversation is, I must go or I will be late."

"Just like that? I fly all the way from Isole dei Re and you walk out on an important conversation because your damn schedule demands it?" How was she going to tell this cold-faced stranger anything, much less the intimate details of her latest doctor's visit?

"Do not swear at me," he said, contriving to sound shocked.

She said a truly foul word. "You mean like that?"

"I do not know what your problem is, but I suggest you get over it. I will be back quite late. If you still feel the need to discuss whatever it is you think is so important, we can talk then."

"And if I don't feel like waiting?"

"You have no choice."

"When have I ever?"

"You made a choice to marry me. No one forced you to speak your vows. If they are chafing now, please remember, you have no one but yourself to blame for your circumstances and I will not tolerate you dismissing your promises or your duty as my wife as easily as you did your duties as a princess this morning."

"They're pretty much the same thing, aren't they?" she asked in a voice filled with angry pain.

"*No.*" His gaze seared her. "You have personal obligations to me that have nothing to do with your responsibility to the crown."

He meant sex, she was sure…but he was wrong. That aspect of their marriage was as wrapped up in her role as princess as everything else. Because it was supposed to result in an heir to the throne and it wasn't going to.

"Maybe I'm feeling unsure about all of my obligations right now."

Fury filled Claudio's gaze, but his voice was controlled and even when he spoke. "I suggest you get sure of them by the time I return to the suite tonight."

"And if I don't?" she dared to taunt.

"Then it will be a very unpleasant night for us both, but I warn you…my weapons are and will always be superior to yours."

"You are so damm arrogant, Claudio." She sighed, her anger draining away. "Anyway, don't be so sure my weapons can't best yours because I have an awful feeling they can."

Her condition and infertility because of it was pretty much nuclear bomb strength when it came to the power necessary to destroy their marriage.

He paled.

"I do not have time for this."

He left.

CHAPTER THREE

THERESE heard the outer door to the suite close with a sense of unreality and then sank onto the edge of the bed, her legs feeling like jelly.

He'd never spelled out for her how little she really meant to him before, but his parting shot pretty much summed up their relationship. He didn't have time for her unless she was playing her role of princess wife to perfection or concubine in his bed.

They'd been married three years and not once had she put her feelings ahead of her duty. The one time she did, he let her know in no uncertain terms that he would not tolerate such behavior from her.

Tears burned a slow path down her cheeks.

She didn't have a marriage. She had a business partnership where she was the junior partner all the way. And the primary partner had no interest in or desire to renegotiate terms. She would fulfill her duties, or else. Only the *or else* in this instance was both permanent and painful. And the thing that hurt the most was that she didn't think it was going to bother him at all.

He would just move on to another businesslike marriage after shattering her heart and not even knowing he'd done it.

"Your Highness, would you like me to order you some dinner?" one of the security men asked from the open doorway.

She averted her face so he could not see the tears, then took a breath to steady her voice. "No, thank you."

"If you are not hungry now, I can order later delivery."

Oh, gosh…she could not handle this. She just wanted to be alone. She forced her convulsing throat to speak. "I do not want any dinner, thank you. And, Roberto, could you…" She had to swallow back a sob.

"Your Highness?"

"Could you please shut the door?"

Her answer was the quiet snick of the door latch catching.

She felt her control slip another notch as the nominal privacy of the shut door registered with her emotions. She'd been holding herself in check for so long; forcing herself to bite back the words of love she'd wanted to utter, to hide her distress at the frequent separations from Claudio brought about by their schedules, and for the past several months pretending that the horrific pain of endometriosis did not exist.

At first, she'd convinced herself it was just the period pain made more intense by going off the pill. But then, one night when Claudio had been gone on yet another business trip, she had fainted from the cramps and when she woke up on the bathroom floor in a pool of blood, she'd known she had to find out what was wrong.

She'd gone to see her doctor in the States, a habit she'd developed early in her marriage to protect her privacy. Trips abroad were easy enough to justify in her schedule that she found it quite easy to hide the purpose of her stop-overs in Miami.

Her doctor's initial prognosis had been utterly disturbing. He'd thought she was probably suffering from endometriosis, but the only way to tell for sure was to perform a laparoscopy. She thought she could handle it and accepted a prescription for painkillers, only to give in the following month and schedule the outpatient surgery.

She'd gotten the results the day before along with a big bucket of ice water to dash her hopes that she would be one of the lucky ones who wasn't impacted too heavily by the disease. Apparently she'd had it for quite a while, but being on the pill had mitigated its effects. There was major tissue build up on both of her ovaries and even with the surgery to remove it all, her chances of getting pregnant without IVF were less than ten percent. Even with IVF, there were no guarantees.

Those were not the kind of odds Crown Prince Claudio had been counting on when he had her take fertility tests before announcing their engagement. A future king had responsibilities to the throne and one of the most important ones was providing an heir to carry on his lineage. He expected her to be able to do that with one hundred percent success and for all intents and purposes, she was infertile.

After seeing the way the press and the Scorsolini family had reacted to Marcello's supposed sterility, Therese knew there was no chance her proud husband would willingly suffer similar vilification for her sake. And she wouldn't expect him to.

If he loved her, it would be different, but then so much would be. Love was not an emotion that could be faked, nor could it be replaced with a sense of duty.

Claudio might offer to remain married, but his heart wouldn't be in it and she could not live with the knowledge that she was a burden around his neck…a source of humiliation to his royal pride.

A sob snaked up from deep inside her to explode out of her mouth and she had to clamp her hand over her lips to keep the sound from traveling to the other room. Feeling like an old woman, she pushed herself to her feet.

She would take a shower…she could at least have privacy for her tears in there.

Once she'd shut the door, then the door on the shower and turned the water on full blast, she cried herself hoarse. She grieved the loss of her marriage, the loss of her hopes of motherhood and stopped fighting the pain that came from loving a man who did not and never would love her.

She ruthlessly quashed any hope that everything would be okay. Deep in her heart, she knew it would not be. After Claudio's reaction to her unexpected departure from her schedule, she didn't even have the tiniest hope that her marriage could or *should* survive this setback.

And that was destroying her. All along, she had harbored the foolish hope that she was wrong, that somehow they could weather the treatment for her condition and the problems it would bring. She hadn't admitted it to herself because it would have hurt too much, but now that she was faced with the final end to her marriage, she had no choice but to acknowledge the living flicker of hope as it died a painful death.

Claudio could not have made it more obvious he did not love her if he had tried. His every action pointed to the carefully defined roles she played in his life, none of them connected to his emotional needs. Unless she counted sex and even if he did…she didn't.

She'd had such hopes when they married. They would make a family and she would know the love she had never known with her parents at least with the children that would come. She had also hoped that eventually Claudio would come to love her. She had wanted it all and now there was nothing but the dead ashes of a fire that had consumed her for almost three years.

She had wanted to be a mother. She'd wanted it so much. Why had he wanted to wait? Why? It wasn't fair. If she had gotten pregnant right away, the endometriosis might never have even shown up. But "if onlys" were as futile as wishing on the moon, an exercise for small children who still believed the possibilities of life were endless.

She had learned they were far too limited. She'd wanted to give birth to the Scorsolini heir and raise him knowing that love lit his path, not duty, that there was more to life than his position. She'd wanted to rectify the mistakes her parents had made with her. She'd wanted a chance at love, knowing that her children would love her, even if their father could never bring himself to do so.

Hadn't she loved her parents, no matter how much they hurt her? And she would have been a good mother, a truly loving mother. She would never have made her children feel they were nothing more than the sum of what they could do for her.

Falling to her knees, she cried, "God in Heaven, it isn't fair!" The words echoed around her in the shower stall, no one there to answer…or if He did, she did not hear the Heavenly voice.

She covered her face and sobbed, but eventually her

tears had to abate. She'd cried herself dry. She turned off the shower, her throat sore and her eyes almost too puffy to see out of. No way would anyone looking at her now and not know how she'd spent the last hour, but it didn't matter. Claudio wouldn't be back for ages and when he did arrive, she planned to be asleep. She was beyond tired, her emotional reserves used up completely.

She hadn't realized how exhausting her pretense of contentment had become until she gave herself permission to let it go. With aching limbs, she pulled on a nightdress and climbed into the bed, not caring that it was just going on seven o'clock.

Without thought, her hand automatically searched out his side of the bed, but of course it was empty. As it had been on so many nights of their marriage and would be every night once she left New York. A dry sob caught in her throat and she bit it back, but she'd soaked her pillow with silent tears before she managed to slip into a fitful sleep. Her last thought that tears were never ending…

She woke sometime later to the sound of the shower going in the bathroom and light spilling from the cracked door into the bedroom. The digital clock beside the bed read nine o'clock. She blinked, trying to think what that meant. It was earlier than she had expected him, but not so early that she could trick herself into thinking he'd rearranged his time for her.

The shower cut off and a minute later, Claudio strolled into the room, completely naked and drying his hair with a white towel. He leaned over to flick his bedside lamp on the lowest setting, casting his bronzed body in a golden glow.

Her mouth went dry as desire and emotional need spiraled low in her belly. It had no place in the devastation inside her and yet it continued to bloom as if her heart had not been decimated in her chest.

He tossed the towel to the side and looked over at her. He paused when her eyes caught his dark gaze. "You are awake."

"You're back."

"Obviously."

She winced at his sarcasm. "How did your meeting go?"

She didn't really care, but nothing else came to mind and total silence simply did not work right then. Nevertheless, she had no doubts that the meeting had gone exactly as he had wanted it to. He was that kind of man. It took a will of iron with the intelligence of Socrates and Einstein combined to defeat Claudio's plans.

Or a woman's rebellious reproductive system, a voice in her head mocked. *He couldn't battle that, no matter how smart and stubborn he was, could he?* And in all likelihood, he wouldn't want to. It would require her having treatments that may or may not be successful for pregnancy that the press was bound to get wind of.

She couldn't bear the thought of what that would mean and knew he wouldn't tolerate such an intrusion into his life.

"It went much as I expected it to."

"I'm not surprised."

"What do you mean by that?"

"Only that you are very good at getting your own way."

"I am not selfish."

"I didn't say you were."

"What *are* you saying?"

"Nothing."

"Roberto said you did not eat dinner."

"I ate on the plane."

Claudio frowned. "A cup of coffee and two cookies is not dinner."

"It was all I wanted."

"Skipping meals is not healthy."

"One missed dinner is not going to kill me."

"Are you sick?" He asked it so baldly, without the slightest trace of compassionate concern that she winced again. "If you are, you should not be traveling."

"Don't worry, I'm not going to give you the flu, or something. I'm not sick." Not with anything he could catch anyway.

He did not look appreciably cheered by that assurance. "I expected you to be awake when I got back, but you were not."

"I had no way of knowing when that would be."

"It is barely nine o'clock." He said it like he couldn't imagine going to bed this early. And probably, he couldn't. The man needed less sleep than anyone she knew.

If he knew she'd gone to bed as early as seven, he'd be convinced she was ill. She saw no reason to enlighten him. "I was tired."

"But you are not sick?"

"No."

"You are certain?"

"Yes."

"Are you pregnant?" He asked the question with the same lack of emotion he'd asked if she was sick to begin with.

The words skewered her. And there was no sense of anticipation in his features, no warming at the prospect, which hurt just like everything else did right then.

"No. Not pregnant," she forced out of stiff lips.

"You are sure?"

She hadn't started, but she was sure. "I'm positive."

"Then this strange behavior is the result of period hormones?"

No doubt a good portion of what she was feeling and her willingness to act on those feelings *was* caused by hormonal imbalances. "If it pleases you to think so, then yes."

Hormone driven, or not, the knowledge her marriage was over was real. His lack of love for her was fact. Her unpredictable reproductive system was not the stuff fantasies were made of and the pain inside her was a physical ache that made it hard to breathe.

He made an impatient movement. "Nothing about this situation pleases me."

"I am sorry."

"I do not want an apology. I want an explanation. You said you had things you wanted to talk about but I come back to the suite only to find you sleeping."

"Is that a crime?"

"No, but you are making no sense to me right now."

"Heaven forbid I should stop fitting in the slot you've assigned me to in your life."

"I have done nothing to deserve your sarcasm."

"Except refuse to listen to me."

"On your timetable. I am here now. Ready to listen." He spread his hands in an expansive gesture that also served to draw her attention back to his beautiful naked body.

Tears burned the back of her eyes, but maybe they were not as never ending as she had thought because no moisture glazed her vision. She was going to miss him so much and it did not even shame her to admit that part of that missing would be pure physical need going unmet. Because for her, the desire was part and parcel to the love and both would be starved of his presence soon enough.

She sighed, trying to breathe through a very different kind of hurt than what had been consuming her body for months now. "I realized that I was foolish to fly up here to talk to you. Waiting three days won't change anything. I'm not even sure there is a point in having the discussion I wanted to have at all."

Really, she just needed to tell him about her condition and then let him work out the details of the separation and divorce. But after her emotional holocaust in the shower, she didn't have the wherewithal to discuss that with him. Her inner reserves were all gone and she simply couldn't face telling him of her failure as a woman, as a wife, especially in the face of his obvious hostility.

"Why is that?" he asked in a dangerously soft undertone she was too drained to understand. Shouldn't he be relieved she didn't want to get all emotional with him?

"Some things cannot be changed." No matter how much she wanted them to be.

"And what are those things?"

"I'd rather not talk about it right now," she admitted in a voice that sounded dodgy to her own ears.

In a move she did not expect, he came around to her side of the bed at supersonic speed and lifted her right out of it. "That is unfortunate because I do."

She gasped and wrapped her arms around his neck to stop herself from falling. "You can't always have your way."

"That is not a concept I recognize."

"Then it's time you did."

He tightened his hold on her. "Stop playing games and tell me what the hell has you acting so far out of character."

The furious undertone in his voice said his patience was about used up. And the iron-hard glint in his brown eyes said he wasn't giving up until she spilled, either. No matter what she wanted, no matter how hard it might be for her, he would settle for nothing less than full disclosure.

She knew it and finally accepted it. She'd started this thing and she had to finish it, no matter how much she might want to put it off. No matter how deeply she might regret her impulsive decision to come to New York. Tears choked her throat and she knew she couldn't begin tell him about her body's deficiency with even a semblance of emotional detachment. There was only one thing she could say.

And she wasn't even sure how to say it.

Feeling pressured beyond endurance in her current overly emotional state and overwhelmed by the simple sensation of being held in his arms for what she was sure was the last time, she ended up just blurting it out, "We have to divorce."

Eyes filling with inimical rage, he dropped her in an act of such utter repudiation her stomach knotted with pain to add on top of all the other hurt she was feeling. If she hadn't grabbed him for support, she would have fallen flat on her bottom.

But he shook her touch off with disdainful rejection. "*You bitch.*"

She'd never seen him so angry and it scared her silly. "I…I h-have to tell you—"

"You will divorce me over my dead body," he interrupted in a deadly voice.

Her mouth opened, but she couldn't make anything come out. She tried, but no words would issue forth. It all hurt too much. She'd never believed she would have to say those fatal words to him. She would have done anything, given any amount of money…even years from her life not to have had to do so. And yet as horrific as his response was to her demand for divorce, she could not make herself speak the truth that labeled her a total failure as a woman.

He had hurt her too much and there was nothing left inside her of trust for his willingness to spare her emotions.

And the harshness of his reaction confused her…made it harder for her to think, to cope with what needed to be said. She simply had not expected him to respond with such fury. After all, they were in effect discussing the dissolution of what he considered a business contract. Nothing more.

For him. For her, it was the end of everything beautiful in her life.

Unless…maybe their marriage was more important to him than she had thought. Could it be true? Could his reaction mean he cared after all? Inside her, her heart leaped…*could she have misread him from the beginning?* All of the evidence she had compiled in her own mind pointed to the fact that she did not matter to him on a personal level, not for who she was—the person inside who craved his love so ardently.

But had she misread it all? She didn't see how she could have. No. She shook her head. It simply wasn't possible. Maybe she could have misread a misspoken phrase here and there, but not an entire lifestyle that continuously pointed out how small a role she played in his life. And nothing could be more convincing than her knowledge of how a Scorsolini male acted in love, because she'd seen it in his younger brothers.

Yet, he was behaving as if the end of their marriage really mattered to him. "Why are you so angry?" she asked in an almost whisper, trying not to let hope build again.

He looked at her in incredulous fury. "You have just told me you want a divorce and you ask me this?"

"Yes." His answer meant so much, she was trembling with fear and anticipation of what it might be.

"I had certain requirements when looking for a wife, you knew this," he gritted from between clenched teeth.

"Y-yes." It was not sounding promising.

"One of those requirements was a wife who understood and accepted the importance of duty and sacrificing one's personal happiness for the sake of what is best for Isole dei Re."

"Were you sacrificing your personal happiness to marry me?" she asked painfully.

She'd always wondered if he'd wanted a different woman, even a different kind of woman. One who was more vivacious and exciting. A woman who would not necessarily make the ideal princess, but who would have matched the fiery passion that bubbled beneath the solid surface of his duty.

"Happiness never came into it one way or the other."

Hurt lancing through her, she said, "It did for me. I was happy to marry you. I wanted you more than I could imagine wanting anyone else."

For some reason, her words made him flinch. "But now you *want* a divorce. Your desire for me, this happiness you mention was short-lived. It did not last even three full years. And yet what did I withhold from you that I promised to give you?"

"Nothing." He had withheld nothing except his love and that had never been on offer as part of their bargain.

"So, you will accept that I have not reneged on my side of our marriage bargain?"

"Yes, I accept it."

"You accept also that you married me with the understanding that it was for a lifetime?"

"Yes, of course."

He moved to tower over her, his fury all the more powerful because he stood there magnificently naked and not in the least bit ashamed of it. "Then you must also accept that I will not allow you to renege on the lifetime commitment you made to me."

"Sometimes things happen that make it impossible to keep a bargain." Even in his vaunted world of business.

"Not in our marriage, they do not."

"They do. They have. I have…" Her throat closed over. She had to say it, but it hurt more than she'd ever expected to say the words out loud.

"Do not say it," he barked. "I will never let you go."

She stared at him. "You don't mean that," she gasped out.

He spun away from her, his whole being vibrating with a palpable rage she still did not understand.

"You will not walk away from our marriage and make me the second sovereign in Scorsolini history to be divorced. Do you understand me?" he bit out in a voice as sharp and frozen as an icicle shard. "I will not allow you to make me a laughingstock amidst my peers and subjects."

Finally she understood. It wasn't his heart being impacted here, it was his pride. He didn't need her…only a whole marriage, because he did not want to look like a fool. Anger welled from deep in her soul. She'd agonized over the prospect of losing him, but all he cared about was how he appeared to the international community.

"Is that all that matters to you? That people might compare you to your father?"

He spun back to face her, his expression a mask of stone. "My father broke his marriage promises. I did not break mine. I will not let you divorce me simply because you want to break yours...*or have already done so*."

The emphasis he gave on the last bit sent chills down her spine and she had to swallow before she answered. "I don't have a choice."

He said a word that made her flinch. "We all have choices, you are making bad ones. You promised me an heir to succeed me on the throne. What about that?" he asked with pure derision.

She almost choked on the pain his demand evoked. She could not give him that heir and his wording reiterated the fact that that alone was her primary requirement as his wife. "I didn't want it to be this way. Please, believe me."

But he looked like he'd rather strangle her than believe her. Even knowing he would never, ever physically hurt her, she found herself stepping backward and away from him.

If possible, his jaw went more rigid.

A knock sounded on the door and she jumped.

"Go away," Claudio barked out.

She'd never heard him use that tone and she knew if she had been the one on the other side of the door, she would have listened, but after a brief pause another knock sounded again. "Your Highness, it is *extremely urgent*."

Claudio said something else vicious under his breath in Italian. Then he grabbed his robe and put the black garment on with jerky movements before stalking over to the door and yanking it open. *"What?"*

She could not make out what the security man said, but she heard the ugly curse that spit forth from her husband's mouth as his body jerked as if receiving a blow.

"Claudio…what is it?" she asked.

But he just shook his head and opened the door wider, obviously planning to leave the room. He stopped on the threshold and looked back over his shoulder, his expression feral. "This is not finished."

The security man gave Claudio a worried look and her a curious one before following his employer to the other room. Therese did not know what to make of either her confrontation with Claudio or what had interrupted it.

And for the second time that night, she stood stock-still in the middle of the bedroom reeling from unenviable emotions after he walked out on her. She did not wonder what could be more important than the end of their marriage because it could be just about anything, she thought sadly. However, she acknowledged that whatever it was, it had to have been singularly important for security to interrupt Claudio against his express wishes.

She walked across the room, feeling like she'd been through World War III and was not quite sure if she was a survivor or not. Yet neither she nor Claudio had actually ever raised their voices. He was incredibly good with undertones, though. No one listening could have doubted how furious he was with her, or how determined he was to keep his marriage for the sake of appearances.

She rubbed her eyes with thumb and forefinger, feeling tired despite the fact she'd woken from what amounted to a longish evening nap and that it still wasn't all that late. She'd been so stupid to think that she meant anything to Claudio on a personal level. His whole reason for wanting to stay married to her had to do with him not being the second Scorsolini sovereign in history to be divorced by his wife.

In his eyes, she had no right or reason to make a

mockery of him in that way. He'd gone to pains to marry a woman who would not do just that very thing. She remembered when he told her about his stepmother divorcing his father.

Therese had been shocked the woman had gone to such extremes. She'd grown up around couples who had stayed married in similar circumstances for the sake of political unity. She realized now why Claudio had liked that reaction so much. Although he'd been absolutely committed to fidelity, saying it was one sin he would find impossible to forgive in either himself or her, he had liked knowing she had been trained to believe that marriage vows were to last a lifetime despite personal differences. Duty came first, last and always.

Which was exactly why she'd asked for a divorce, but he didn't know that. Once he did, he would grasp for an end to their marriage grabbing a divorce with both hands.

Therese slowly sank into one of the armchairs in the corner, weariness overcoming her.

She could not have handled the confrontation with him worse if she had tried. Instead of telling him of her condition and almost certain infertility, she had told him they had to divorce. While that might well be true, it *was not* the first thing she should have said to him.

He thought she'd brought up divorce because she wanted one, which could not be farther from the truth, but duty dictated she let go of the man she loved for both his greater good and that of his country. His final words before they were interrupted had said it all. He needed heirs. She could not guarantee providing them. The odds of conceiving were not good enough for a future king.

Those facts left her dreams in shambles around her feet.

Why was life so hard? What had she done wrong to bring this kind of misery on herself? Her doctor had said it wasn't personal, that endometriosis happened to lots and lots of women, but it felt personal to her.

Especially when the results of the disease were ripping her life apart into big jagged patches of pain and more pain.

And that was her only excuse for the way she'd handled the news. She was hurting so much, her usual diplomacy had completely deserted her. Her father would be so ashamed, but then he'd never been overly impressed with her to begin with.

In his eyes, she'd always had two strikes against her... she'd been born female and she had no interest in politics. No matter how pleased Mother had been, the fact that Therese had ended up married to a crown prince meant nothing to her father. He would have been happier if she had gone to the right schools, made friends with the right people and pursued American politics. Then she would have been of benefit to *him*.

Regardless of Claudio's influence in world politics, she could not personally significantly benefit her father who had moved on to a diplomatic position in South America. He therefore considered her useless to him and let her know it in all the subtle ways he had been employing since her childhood.

Psychologists said that women often married men like their fathers and she'd been determined not to. She had always believed that she had succeeded in marrying a man very different, but now she realized she'd done exactly what she'd sworn not to. She'd married a man who was no more enamored of her person than her father was.

Looking back over almost three years of marriage, she

saw that Claudio employed a subtle means of letting her know the insignificance of her place in his life as well. She simply hadn't seen the road signs for what they were because she so desperately wanted them to say something else. Because he had needed her in the most basic ways—sexually and as an adjunct to his position—she had believed he had more feelings for her than her dad did.

She couldn't even blame him for deceiving her, the delusion had been entirely self-perpetuating. But acknowledging that did not make the pain of realization any less.

Talk about being an idiot. She had that role down to an art and admitting it hurt almost as much as Claudio's rejection.

And his attitude had been nothing less than that. He wanted to keep their marriage intact, but only for the sake of his own pride and for the baby he expected her to give him. Not because he wanted to keep her as his wife. Not because she meant anything to him.

She shivered, her entire body shaking violently and she realized she was very cold. It was a chill that came from deep inside, but nevertheless she got up and pulled the blanket from the bed to wrap up in as if it might help. It didn't.

Feeling so torn apart standing was not an option, she sat back down in the armchair…and waited.

Claudio had said it was not over and as much as she had no desire to continue their confrontation, she had no doubt that was exactly what would happen when he came back. And no matter how much it might hurt to give, or how angry his pride filled responses made her…she owed him an explanation.

She didn't know how long she sat there, thoughts skittering through her brain. It could have been a few minutes, or as long as an hour, but at some point he came back into the room, his expression one she had never seen on his face before.

"Get dressed."

CHAPTER FOUR

"WHAT? Why?" Was he kicking her out of the suite because she'd asked for a divorce? No, that made no sense.

"We have to fly back to Lo Paradiso immediately."

She jumped up from the chair, holding the blanket tight around her like a shield. "Is something wrong?"

"My father had a heart attack."

"No." Not King Vincente. "How bad is he?"

"He is stable, but requires a bypass surgery. He is in the hospital," Claudio gritted out, his eyes accusing. "He is alone, without any family around him because you saw fit to fly up here for no good reason."

"Where is your brother?"

"On his way now that I have called him. Papa refused to have him called and allowed me to be contacted only after he had stabilized. Had you been there, this would never have happened."

She gasped. "You cannot blame me for him having a heart attack."

"No, but had you been there, you would have contacted my brothers and myself despite my father's wishes. He could not have ordered you like a servant."

"Are you sure about that?" Perhaps the king would not

have ordered her compliance like that of an employee, but she cared for him and might well have acquiesced for the sake of his stress levels.

But then she acknowledged, she would have somehow managed to do what she thought was best…which would probably have been to call Claudio. She, and the rest of the family, were used to relying on him in a crisis. Indeed, her first reaction when she had started having pain in her lower abdomen had been to tell Claudio, to ask for his help dealing with it.

She had decided against that course of action out of a need to protect him.

"Yes, I am certain. You would have contacted me, even if Papa had not known you had done it," Claudio said, showing he knew her well in almost every way but the one that counted most to her.

He did not know of her love for him and could not care less about its existence, she painfully admitted to herself.

"You have been contacted now," she pointed out.

"What if he had died? What if it is worse than he told me that it is?"

"I could not have controlled either of those outcomes and I have no doubt you have spoken to the doctor already and know exactly the extent of your father's illness."

"I have and it is not good. You should have been there," he repeated as if that betrayal was as bad as her request for a dissolution to their marriage.

"You're not being fair. You know I felt I had to come. I needed to talk you."

"About breaking your promises to me. And yet you had already decided before I returned to the hotel suite tonight that the discussion could wait. What was so imperative was not really that important to you at all. You left on a selfish whim and my father paid because of it. I made a huge miscalculation when I asked you to marry me," he said in a final slash of derision.

However, she was too inured by her own anger at his reaction to the news of his father's illness to experience the pain his words would have caused a few short hours ago. "I can see how you might think that way," she said with a sigh. "But there are things I still have to tell you."

"I do not want to hear them."

"You need to."

The disdain in his expression said it all. He was listening to her explanations when hell froze over. "I am leaving here in ten minutes. If you wish to go with me, be dressed."

Therese spent the first two hours of the flight between New York and Lo Paradiso simmering with anger. She'd taken a seat as far away from him as possible when they boarded the plane and hadn't even cared when he showed every sign of being content with that fact. A one word description of his behavior came to mine and it was anything but complimentary.

When had she ever given Claudio cause to believe that she was flighty or selfish? She had fulfilled her duty as princess, dismissing her personal needs time and again, but apparently two years as the perfect diplomat's daughter and political ally had gone up in smoke with one act he did not approve of.

Didn't she, as his wife, deserve even a little understanding in that regard? But he'd made it clear…she was a princess, first, last and always to him. Her role of wife was always overshadowed by her primary role as his future queen. The knowledge shredded what was left of her feminine ego.

She had shown the temerity to reorganize her schedule for something she felt was important and he had gone ballistic. Not only that, he just assumed that her reasons for saying they needed to divorce had to be spurious and selfish ones. Why? She had given him everything she had to give as his wife, even if he had not realized it. When had she ever made any choice related to him out of selfishness? Even her decision to marry him had been made with the knowledge that she could be the kind of wife he wanted.

She had loved him, but she would not have married him knowing he did not love her if she had believed she would not be the right kind of wife for him. Looking back at how much she had agonized over what was best for him and how little time she had spent worrying on her own behalf, she wondered if she was some kind of masochist or a real idiot, or both.

But then she'd spent her whole life trying to please other people. First her parents, each of whom had a different agenda for her life. She'd fulfilled her mother's because it had seemed the only one she had a chance at succeeding at.

Mother had said time and again that Therese's beauty and poise were her greatest assets, that she was to play those assets carefully. That had been easy to do. The physical beauty was a gift of Providence and the poise was something that no diplomat's daughter could survive her school years without.

Those attributes had won Claudio's attention, but even her perfect manners and political savvy added in had not been enough to sway him toward the marriage vote. He'd wanted to be sure she would not disappoint him in bed and had tested her on that score.

She remembered Maggie saying Tomasso had done the same thing. Not in those exact words, of course, but she'd known what the other woman meant. After all, Therese knew these Scorsolini men. She'd been shocked by Tomasso's behavior only because it had been so obvious to her from the beginning that he really cared about Maggie.

He loved her and no one in the family could doubt that fact. Not now. Not ever, in her opinion.

But Claudio did not and had not loved Therese when he had been courting her with an eye for marriage. He'd kissed her and touched her with searing passion, evoking a response that she had learned to accept, but which had at first shocked and terrified her. To be so at mercy to her body's desires had gone against her need for control and the way she had been raised to suppress any deep emotion.

Truthfully she would probably never have allowed her love for Claudio to bloom fully if he had not evoked her latent sensuality. It had broken through her every emotional barrier and laid her heart bare to his influence.

Now she would pay the price for her weakness.

Vulnerability always came with a cost. Hadn't her father told her that time and again, and her mother…though in different words? Yet, she'd been powerless to stop herself falling in love with the prince who had a heart made of stone.

The cost of that love was her own shattered heart.

Learning of King Vincente's illness had added another level of pain to the maelstrom of hurt inside of her. She loved her father-in-law in a way she'd never been free to care for her own father. But then King Vincente had accepted her as her father had not. He admired her feminine strength and told her so. He enjoyed her company and told her that as well.

He commented on his son's dedication to duty in less than complimentary ways when he thought she was being neglected. He had been her ally for three years and if she lost him to death, it would tear her apart. It would also mean her husband's need for an heir would be even greater.

Claudio had said the older man was stable, but she knew how unpredictable a heart condition could be. And no one had even known that King Vincente had suffered from one. As unfair as she'd felt Claudio's accusations about her behavior had been, if she had known her father-in-law's health was at risk, she *would* have waited for her husband's return from New York to talk about their marriage.

Because she cared too much for King Vincente, who was a better father to her than her blood relative to have ever allowed for the possibility that he might end up alone in a hospital room worried for his life.

Her own fears in that regard were enough to make her heart quake. On top of that, she was still reeling from the way Claudio had smashed her every hope that she meant anything more to him than a body in his bed and a political sidekick of the necessary sex.

She honestly did not think she could stand an ongoing war of silent hostility with her husband in addition to everything else. Though once she explained about her endometriosis at least that would end. He might be bitterly disappointed. He might even see her as a complete feminine failure, as she did herself, but he would no longer be furious with her.

Her own anger said she should not care, but her heart was too bloody from recent wounds to withstand much more and she was smart enough to realize it. Besides, it was entirely possible she would not be able to hide her physical agony from the endometriosis when her monthly came.

At least if she told him about it now, she would not have to deal with revelations during a time she was least up to doing so. Every month got worse and until she had the surgery, it would continue to do so. While he might not like hearing the truth, it couldn't be worse than his belief that she was selfishly letting him down.

She moved to sit beside him, anger and the need for honesty between them still at war inside of her. "Claudio."

He looked at her, his dark eyes winter-cold. "What?"

Remember, diplomacy and tact, she told herself. "I don't want to add to the burden of worry you are dealing with King Vincente, but—"

"Then do not."

"What?" she asked, not having expected to be cut off like that. After all, despite the way he'd been acting earlier, he'd been trained in diplomacy since infancy, too.

"You are about to tell me why you want a divorce, are you not?"

"Yes."

"Do not."

"But I need to."

"I do not wish to hear it."

"But—"

"You can have your divorce, Therese, but not until my father's health is stable enough to withstand news that his treasured daughter-in-law has feet of clay. Until that point, we will continue the facade of our marriage. *Capice?*"

"No, not really. I don't understand at all, actually," she admitted, reeling for the third time that night at a totally unexpected reaction from him. It was as if he had become a completely different man to the one she had thought she married. "I thought you said our marriage would end over your dead body."

"I have changed my mind."

"I can see that, but why?"

"You are not the only one who has grown bored with the setup, but I would have done nothing about it which I am sure you think makes me a fool for duty."

And she had thought she had grown inured to more pain. What a joke. She felt like her heart was being ripped right out of her chest. "I never said I was bored."

"But I am." He flicked his hand in a throwaway gesture that implied their marriage meant that little to him. "The truth is, I am only too happy to give you a divorce, but as I said…it will have to wait on my father's health. You can live with that limitation, I imagine?"

"You *want* a divorce?" she asked, that portion of his words the only ones that registered with any real impact.

This was worse than any scenario she could have predicted. She'd thought it was very possible he might accept her solution with an equanimity that would hurt, but she had never envisioned he would actually welcome it. That he had grown *bored* being married to her.

"You are beautiful, Therese, but a man needs something more than a pretty face and impeccable table manners to ease the prospect of an entire lifetime together. Once you started turning me down in the bedroom, your stock in my life dropped dangerously low. As I said, I would have stuck it out because once I make a promise, I keep it. But I will not fight for a marriage I do not actually want."

"You don't want to be married to me?" she asked faintly, needing him to verify his words.

"Why so surprised? You feel the same way."

"I…do?" she asked stupidly, her brain having ceased to function on an analytical level.

"And you did not even have the strength of character to stick it out," he said, treating her words like a confirmation rather than a question. "Funny, I always thought there was more to you than that, but I will not pretend grief I do not feel."

"But earlier…"

"I allowed my pride to dictate my words. Certainly I was not reacting to what I really wanted."

Feeling sick to her stomach from some very real grief, Therese lurched up from her seat. "Then, I guess there is nothing left to say."

"Nothing that I could want to hear, no."

She nodded jerkily, amazed on one level at how much agony the human heart could withstand without ceasing to beat and simply hemorrhaging internally from that pain on another.

Claudio watched his wife stumble down the aisle back to her original seat and wanted to hit something. Damn it, why did she have to look so distraught? She was the one who had asked for a divorce. She was the one who had found someone else.

And she'd wanted to tell him about it. As if hearing the details could somehow make her infidelity all right.

She was probably going to tell him that she had fallen in love, that she couldn't help herself. He'd heard that line used before by friends and acquaintances in the world he moved within. But rarely did even the love vote move those people in positions of major political impact to divorce.

He had understood his stepmother's need to leave his

father, but he'd never understood her going so far as to get a divorce. It wasn't as if she had ever remarried…and one time early on he'd overheard her tell someone she probably never would. So, why get a divorce, why drag the royal family's name through the mud.

For a principle?

He'd been so damn sure Therese would never do anything so rash, but he had not accounted for her finding someone else.

Perhaps arrogantly, he had assumed he was enough for her both in and out of bed. He had been wrong. So why was she acting like his words devastated her?

He'd said them to save face. They'd come bursting out, totally unexpected, when he'd realized she was about to tell him all about the other man. He wasn't proud of lying. He was an honest man and that shamed him, but he would not unspeak the words if he could.

His pride had been lacerated by her request for a divorce and the subsequent realization that his every niggling fear about her lack of sexual interest and ditzy woolgathering had been justified. She had found someone else and she wanted to divorce him, Principe Claudio Scorsolini, for this other man.

There was no other explanation possible for the night's revelations.

The knowledge made him furious enough to want to kill, but it wasn't her he wanted to hurt. It was the man who had lured his gentle wife to a passion that had obviously surpassed what they found together.

Claudio could barely believe that was possible.

The biggest lie he had told Therese was that he had grown bored with her. He continued to crave her body, even with her lack of recent sexual availability. In fact, it had challenged him as much as they had frustrated him. It was the natural predator in him, but having her move away had drawn him inexorably into chasing her.

The knowledge that he had planned seductions and had put so much effort into claiming her body when she had been pining for someone else made him sick with anger. Even so, he could not believe he had said what he did to her. Not because he wasn't capable of being as ruthless as any of his ancestors who had settled Isole dei Re, but because the words had been so far from the truth. He was shocked he had come up with that line of defense.

Their marriage had never been only about the sex, though it had been a big issue for him. For what man wouldn't it be? But she'd believed him. Which said what about how she saw him? He had been nothing more to her than a body in her bed and a way to fulfill her mother's ambitious social climbing nature.

So who was the new guy? Not a nobody that was for sure. An American. That would make sense of her frequent trips to the States. It shouldn't be too hard for his private investigator Hawk to find a name. For some reason, the idea of getting details on his own did not grind in his gut like broken glass like the thought of having her tell him did. Maybe because he felt in control when he was the one garnering the information.

What Claudio would do with that data once he got hold of it, he was not sure.

The desire for revenge was a bloodlust inside him.

Would he ruin the other man? Would he do anything to prevent the chances of Therese finding happiness with him? All he had to do was refuse the divorce. It was no easy thing to end a marriage to a member of the royal family of Isole dei Re.

Flavia had only succeeded with his father because the marriage had taken place in Italy, and even in that case because he had not contested the divorce or denied her charge of infidelity. She had no physical evidence to make a case with, but Papa had felt so much guilt over letting down his own high moral standards, he had let his wife walk away.

Claudio did not know if he had the same fortitude. He had told Therese that he would not cling to a relationship he did not want. That was truth…but it was not true that he did not want his marriage. He didn't know if he could touch her again, knowing her body had belonged to another man, but he did not know if he could let her go, either.

And the knowledge galled him, making him feel even more vicious than learning of her unfaithfulness.

They arrived in Lo Paradiso sometime after one in the morning and went directly to the hospital.

Therese had tried to doze on the plane, but she'd found it impossible to sleep with her thoughts careening from the shock of Claudio's expressed desire for a divorce and King Vincente's heart attack. She had believed that nothing could be worse than learning she had endometriosis with a high chance of total infertility.

She had been wrong. Finding out she had no option but to let Claudio go had hurt, but discovering he wanted out… that he was bored with her had destroyed her. She no longer had any doubts about whether or not she was a survivor of their private war. She knew she had not survived, that her heart was dead inside her.

Only if it was dead, why did it still hurt so much?

When they arrived at the hospital, Claudio grabbed her arm to stop her from stepping out of the limousine. "Therese..."

She didn't look at him. She couldn't. "What?"

"My family is under enough stress right now."

"Yes." So was she, but he'd made it painfully clear he didn't care about that.

She'd had the audacity to ask for a divorce and that made her persona non grata where he was concerned.

"I do not want them further distressed by news of our imminent breakup."

Did he have to put it that way, as if he couldn't wait to be rid of her? "Of course."

"I expect you to behave as you always have toward me."

"I'm sure we will have no trouble maintaining the status quo." She glared at him. "It's not as if we have a marriage like your brothers. No one expects us to be affectionate."

She shook his hand off with an angry jerk and stepped out of the car, her public mask firmly in place. Then, showing that she had indeed been raised by a mother who had drilled her to the point where she had once sat out the whole second half of a girls basketball game in the sixth grade with a broken ankle rather than cry in public and let the coach know the extent of her injury, she waited for Claudio so she could walk with him into the hospital.

It was expected of her. She would do her part to display the outward appearance of solidarity. She directed her gaze straight ahead, her body only a few inches from his, but it might as well have been a mile.

How many times had she walked beside him and wished he would put his arm around her or take her hand...to show her in some way that he felt the connection between them?

But he never did. It made her furious with herself, but she wished for that physical support even more right now.

She had no idea what they would find inside that hospital and she was scared, her heart bleeding and battered from all sides.

They walked toward the building through a barrage of noisy reporters and flashing cameras.

One man broke through the security barrier and got right into her face. "What will it mean to you if King Vincente dies, Princess Therese? Are you looking forward to being queen?"

She put her hand up and averted her face, but her feet faltered and she had to force herself to keep moving. The insensitivity of the question shouldn't have surprised her. She knew how intrusive the press could be, but she was in no way up to handling that thoughtlessness right now. She did her best to hide it, but she flinched when another reporter got close with a flashing camera.

Suddenly Claudio's big body was there, shielding her from the reporters, his arm strong around her shoulders and his voice barking orders at the security team to do a better job at keeping the paparazzi away.

Despite feeling like she was leaning on the enemy, she turned into the comfort his human shield offered and let him lead her past the clamoring reporters and continuously flashing camera bulbs. She couldn't help thinking it would be like this, or worse if the press got wind of her inability to get pregnant without IVF. What kind of rotten questions and accusations would they throw at her and Claudio then?

It didn't bear thinking about. Not if she wanted to maintain her sanity in the face of her fear for King Vincente's health.

Once they were inside the hospital and the solid steel door had closed behind them, Claudio let her go as if he could not stand being close to her for another second.

They walked down the hospital hallways in silence. The head of the hospital himself came to meet them and lead them to the waiting area designated for King Vincente's family. He and Claudio talked, but when she realized he was saying nothing she hadn't heard before about her father-in-law's condition, she tuned the two men out.

Somewhere within these quiet walls, her father-in-law lay in a bed fighting for his life. Stabilized, or not, his condition was what could hardly be termed safe if a bypass surgery was necessary. She'd read of people, perfectly healthy people dying of a second heart attack before the surgery could be performed. She could only give thanks that the first one had not killed the country's ruler.

CHAPTER FIVE

MAGGIE came rushing to Therese the moment she and Claudio walked through the archway that led to the waiting room.

The other woman took one look at her and grabbed Therese, hugging her hard. "It's going to be all right. He needs a bypass as I'm sure you know, but he's a strong man. He'll be fine."

Therese let her sister-in-law hold her, pathetically grateful for the human contact that was not motivated by a need to put on a facade for the press. "I don't know what I'll do if he dies," she whispered.

She hadn't meant to say the words and shocked herself silly doing so. She was so used to protecting her feelings, it was second nature, but her emotions were too close to the surface to be completely hidden.

"He won't die, sweetie. Don't talk that way." Maggie patted Therese's back like she was comforting a child and she felt tears slide into her eyes.

She could not remember the last time someone had acknowledged she had feelings. Had touched her to comfort her. Certainly not Claudio. He acted as if her heart was made of iron ore and twice as hard as it should be.

Her parents had never even comforted her as a child. She was supposed to hide her every fear and never admit to pain. Hence the basketball game that had led to a week in traction as payment for the folly of not expressing her pain in any way.

She pulled away from Maggie, knowing that if she didn't, the other woman's compassion would be her undoing. "Can we see him?"

"Tomasso is with him now. He's sleeping, but you can look in on him." She bit her lip. "He looks pale, but he's doing fine. Really."

Therese nodded and then turned to go to King Vincente's room, not waiting to see if Claudio followed. He did, the presence of his tall frame beside her obvious to her senses even though he was not in her line of sight and was walking as silently as a Black Ops agent. There was a connection between them that she doubted divorce and the separation of an ocean and a continent could even sever…on her side anyway.

She pushed the door open to the room, quietly stepping inside.

A dim light was on behind the bed and the king lay, unmoving, his normally bronzed features the color of flour paste except for the dark, bruising circles under his eyes.

"He looks so weak." Claudio's voice from right beside her was hoarse with emotion.

"Yes, but he will be fine," Tomasso said from nearby.

And Therese found herself praying, *Please, Lord, let him be fine*.

Tomasso moved to stand beside his brother and whisper, "You must have gotten an immediate takeoff slot at the airport to get here so quickly."

Claudio shrugged. "It was necessary."

"They have scheduled the surgery for tomorrow morning."

"Marcello and Danette should be here by then."

"Yes. Flavia as well."

"She is coming?"

"Danette called her with the news as soon as she heard and Flavia wanted to fly out with them."

"Will Danette be all right on the long flight?" Claudio asked with genuine concern.

Envy that made Therese feel small and mean twinged through her.

Tomasso smiled, though it wasn't up to his usual wattage. "According to Marcello, she insists that she is pregnant, not ill. Maggie says the same."

"Maggie is certainly ill with her pregnancy. I am surprised you let her fly over."

Tomasso sighed, his expression a mix of emotions that hurt Therese to see because it was so obvious his wife's distress truly mattered to him. "There was no stopping her, but I wish to take her back to the palace for some rest soon."

"Yes." Claudio moved a step closer to his father's bed and reached out to touch the older man's arm. "It is a good thing Danette's morning sickness is not so acute."

They were so patently not the words he was thinking that Therese felt a sudden constriction in her throat.

"He is going to be fine. Believe it, Claudio," Tomasso said, showing he was not fooled by his brother's comment, either.

Claudio said nothing, his attention focused entirely on his father's still form in the bed.

Tomasso patted his brother on the shoulder and left the room.

Therese moved to stand beside Claudio and laid her

hand against King Vincente's cheek. It was warm to the touch and that gave her comfort. No matter how pale he looked, his heart was pumping life's blood through his body. They stood that way for few minutes, both of them touching the man in the bed, but not touching each other.

Then Therese dropped her hand from King Vincente's face and moved to the other side of the room to pray, her pleas that went Heavenward filled with an uncertain faith. Tomasso returned and whispered something to Claudio. Claudio nodded and said something back and the other man left again.

He caught her gaze. "Tomasso and Maggie are going back to the palace. He wants her to rest and she will not go without him."

"I'm glad he's willing to go then."

"I told him you would go as well."

"I would rather stay here."

"That is my place."

"It is mine, too."

"Not after tonight."

She felt like he'd slapped her. "I love King Vincente. You know that. I want to stay here with you."

"You need your rest," Claudio replied, about as movable as a rock wall.

"I won't sleep. I couldn't."

"Do not be a fool, child. Go home and come back in the morning." The raspy voice came from the bed and Therese's knees almost buckled when she heard it.

She crossed the floor in a rush and took the hand that did not have an IV in it in her own. "King Vincente…"

"How many times…" He paused, taking a couple of shallow breaths. "Told you to call me Papa."

"I—"

"Surely that is not too much to ask," Claudio said in a controlled voice she knew masked an anger he did not want his father to guess at.

She'd never felt comfortable calling the older man Papa, but now even more than before…it would feel wrong. Soon she would be gone from their family completely.

Yet, how could she deny him such a simple request? The answer was: she couldn't. "I'm sorry, Papa, but I want to stay with you."

"You need your rest."

"I need to stay with you."

"Do not argue with him, he is sick."

"I know that, but I also know you're only bringing it up to get your own way," she accused her stubborn husband.

King Vincente laughed weakly, his blue eyes dulled by fatigue. "That is my daughter-in-law. She is a perfect match for my son."

The words hurt because according to Claudio, she was no match at all, but Therese forced a smile. "Please, won't you let me stay with you?"

"There are things my son and I must discuss. Just in case. I will not rest afterward if I am worried about you not getting your rest."

"Don't talk like you are going to die, *please*."

"We must all face death sooner, or later, child."

"But I want it to be later. Tomasso said you will be fine. The doctors said so."

The king shrugged, the casually confident movement at odds with his frail appearance. "The surgery has a very high success rate, but there is always a risk in things like this. It will be as God wills."

"I don't believe it is your time."

"Neither do I, *cara*, but it would be remiss of me not to settle last minute issues with my heir."

Therese looked to Claudio. She did not know why. He was no longer her champion…if he ever had been. Certainly she could not expect any sort of comfort from that direction, but she'd gotten used to relying on him.

Their eyes met and his dark gaze held…nothing. She blinked and turned her head, unable to deal with that as she all at once realized that while their marriage had not been the love match of the century, there had been intimacy. She recognized it only now that it was gone.

Always before when their gazes met, she had seen a recognition of herself and her place in his life in his eyes. To see nothing of the kind now made her realize that perhaps there had been more to her marriage than she had thought, but whatever there had been—it was gone now.

"Go home and rest. I will it," King Vincente said, managing to sound arrogant and in charge even in his weakened state.

She had no trouble seeing how he had kept news of his heart attack from his sons until he desired it to reach them.

"I will leave," she said, knowing he would take the words for acquiescence. But she'd lived enough years around politicians to know how to appear to make a promise without doing anything of the kind.

She would leave…the hospital room.

"Good."

She leaned down and kissed both his cheeks. "Be well, Papa. For all our sakes."

"I will do my best."

She forced another smile. "I'm sure you will."

She could not make herself meet Claudio's gaze again. "See you later," she said in his direction and walked from the room.

She went directly to the waiting room where she knew she would find the others and she sent Tomasso and Maggie on their way. Maggie was dead on her feet and it didn't take much persuasion to get Tomasso to leave so his pregnant wife could be put to bed.

Therese took up residence in the waiting room, having the small comfort that if King Vincente took a turn for the worse, this time she would be on the spot. She curled up on the sofa and watched the television sightlessly as it created a sort of white noise to the background of her unhappy thoughts.

She woke up to the sound of voices. Claudio, his brother Marcello, his wife Danette and Flavia were talking in hushed tones as if trying not to wake her.

Therese sat up. A suit jacket that had been placed over her like a blanket fell off one shoulder. Claudio's scent and warmth from his coat surrounded her, comforting her when it should do anything but in the current situation. He must have found her here earlier and covered her.

He turned to face her, even though she'd made no sound. His face was an impenetrable mask. "You did not go back to the palace."

"I never said I would."

"You said you would leave."

"I did." She looked away from his regard, no more capable of dealing with this new remote Claudio than she had been earlier. "The hospital room."

"But not the hospital."

"No."

"Why not?"

"I wanted to be here in case something else happened."

"You knew Papa and I assumed you would leave with Tomasso."

She shrugged, dislodging the suit coat further. "I am not responsible for assumptions brought about by two men's arrogant belief that the rest of the world will fall in with their plans simply because they say so."

Flavia chuckled. "That is telling him, Therese. Do not let this bossy son of mine believe he rules you completely."

"There is no chance of that, Mamacita."

Therese was fairly certain she was the only one who heard the harsh undertone in Claudio's voice, but to her ears it was as loud as if he'd shouted out how much he disliked her.

"I am glad to hear it. You are far too much like your papa, believing you control the world around you and everyone in it. Life does not work that way, as I am sure Vincente is realizing for perhaps the first time."

"He is more than aware, I assure you," Claudio said, his voice now subdued.

"And you, my son?"

"Content yourself with knowing that he and I are both aware how little our will carries the day."

Flavia's face softened with concern. "I am sorry, Claudio. Times like this are difficult, but Vincente will be fine. Believe it."

"I hope you are right."

"I am always right, it is just the males of this family are slow catching on sometimes."

Danette laughed out loud while both Scorsolini brothers smiled wryly. Neither one would hurt the older woman by arguing with her, but both were too arrogant to believe anyone else ever knew better than they did. It was all Therese could do not to blurt out that Flavia had been wrong about one thing.

Like King Vincente, she had always believed that Therese and Claudio were the perfect match and had been vocal in saying so. Once his father's health could withstand the blow, Claudio would make sure everyone knew just how wrong both his parents had been.

Flavia said, "I would like to see Vincente."

"Yes, of course," Claudio replied. "He is sleeping now, but may waken again. He will be glad to find you by his bedside."

Marcello nodded. "I will stay as well."

"In that case, I shall see our wives to the palace. It appears that is the only way I can be assured that Therese will return to rest."

"When is the surgery scheduled for?" Therese asked, ignoring the barb and doing a fair job of avoiding his gaze while making it appear she was looking at him.

"Five hours from now."

"I want to be here."

"Then you will return with me now to the palace and get at least some semblance of rest beforehand."

If there were shares in the bossy market, he had a stranglehold on them. "I don't need you telling me what to do."

"I'd prefer to stay here with Marcello and Flavia," Danette said before Claudio could answer.

Marcello gently put his arm around her slightly thickened waist and pulled her close, kissing her temple. "You are pregnant, *cara mia*, you need to rest for both your sake and that of our unborn child. Please do me the favor of returning to the palace with my brother."

Therese wondered if Claudio would ever have been as tender with her...even if she had been pregnant. A tiny voice inside her heart said it wouldn't have mattered. She would have had her dreams with, or without he extra bit of tender care. Seeing her deepest wish living out fulfillment in another woman's body brought a poignant pain that had nothing to do with envy.

She adored Danette and wanted only the best for her, but Therese could no more stifle the urgent longing inside herself for a child than she could pretend that Claudio loved her.

Danette turned in Tomasso's arms and kissed him on the lips, right there in front of the rest of the family and he did not even sort of flinch. "If that's what you really want, all right. But are you sure you don't want me here as moral support?"

"Thank you, *mi precioso*. Your offer is appreciated, but I will feel better knowing you are taking care of yourself." Then *he* kissed *her,* putting enough enthusiasm into the effort to show that he was not in the least embarrassed by the public show of affection from his wife.

Therese could not help comparing the way Danette and Marcello interacted with the way that she and Claudio did. She would never have dared to kiss him in something as public as a hospital waiting room. She'd never even kissed him in front of any of his family members in the private apartments of the palace.

Looking back, she realized that in three years, she could probably count on one hand the number of times she had kissed him when they were not already in the process of making love. She had never felt the confidence to instigate lovemaking, but she had always responded...with more passion than she had believed possible.

He'd praised her for it, but now she wondered if she had been too enthusiastic. He'd grown bored with her… because she'd been too easy?

And even before he had told her he had grown bored with her, she'd known he hadn't felt anything tender toward her like his brothers did for their wives.

She looked at Marcello and Danette, so close they were obviously two halves of the same whole and an ache seared Therese's heart. She would never know that kind of love because she knew she would never stop loving Claudio, even if right now she disliked him almost as much as she loved him.

Her future stretched out like a bleak, lonely wasteland ahead of her.

What was wrong with her that she did not inspire love in the people who were supposed to hold affection for her? Her parents had only ever seen her as a means to an end or a sore disappointment and Claudio had given her only a marginally more important role in his life. That of lover and helpmate, but he was only too happy to snatch it away.

Danette's parents adored her, if they were a bit overprotective. Therese had seen that at the wedding. What did the other woman have that was so lacking in herself?

Envy was a sin that she had always been determined never to feel, but as she looked on at her sister-in-law so obviously loved and pregnant with the child Therese craved but would never have, she ached so badly for those things herself that her teeth hurt. She would die rather than see them taken from the sweet Danette, but was not sure her own life was worth a counterfeit dollar without them.

She surged to her feet, needing to get out of there and the suit coat fell to the floor. She bent down and grabbed it and then held it out in Claudio's general direction. "Here."

He took it, his fingers brushing her own and she yanked her hand back, stumbling against the couch as her body instinctively retreated as well.

"Therese, are you all right, child?" Flavia asked, her voice laced with concern.

"Fine. J-just tired," Therese choked out, her eyes burning with tears that were only partially linked to the man lying so fragile in a hospital bed down the corridor. "I'll wait in the car."

And dismissing etiquette for the first time in her adult life, she rushed from the room without a single farewell to any of its occupants.

Therese was like a quiet wraith sitting on the seat beside Danette during the car ride to the palace. She spoke only in response to questions from Danette. Claudio, she ignored entirely. Luckily his family had already decided she'd taken his father's ill health hard and he did not think her behavior would give rise to speculation on his sister-in-law's part.

But when Therese had gone rushing from the waiting room, he'd had to convince his stepmother not to follow her. He had suspected that her distress had not been centered solely on his father's condition and he hadn't wanted to take the risk of his family finding that out.

She'd refused to meet Claudio's gaze for the past few hours. He didn't know what she'd seen when she'd looked to him for solace in his father's hospital room. He'd been certain that his anger toward her did not show because he had not wanted to upset his father. Yet, something she had seen in his eyes had upset her to the point that she had looked away with an expression on her face that made him want to grab her and hold her, no matter how stupid that desire made him feel.

After that, she did not look at him again…not then and not later.

If the prospect of imminent divorce was so upsetting, then why the hell had she asked for one? Or was the reality of her perfidy coming home to roost?

She was beloved by both his parents and he knew they would be hurt deeply if there was to be a divorce. Particularly if they were to discover that Therese had betrayed her wedding vows. She adored both his father and his mother and would not want to see either hurt by her actions.

Was she finally starting to realize what the result of those actions would be?

Pity she hadn't considered it before becoming involved with another man. Just thinking of her with someone else made him feel murderous and he had to bite back angry questions he would rather be boiled in oil than ask in front of Danette. Was Therese regretting that involvement now? Was she counting the cost now that it was too late, wishing she had not asked for the divorce? Or was he merely engaged in wishful thinking?

Perhaps it *was* simple worry for his father that had upset her so much, but Claudio had never once seen her as lacking in control as she had been when she'd practically run from the hospital room. And he could not get past the fact she still would not look at him.

His jacket smelled of her…a soft floral scent that had the power to drive him mad with need.

His muscles were rigid with the desire to reach out and take her in his arms. Not that he would have done so in the circumstances, even if she had not asked for a divorce and confirmed his worst suspicions. He did not engage in public displays of affection. His dignity as future sovereign on the Scorsolini throne demanded he be circumspect in his dealings with his wife.

But seeing his younger brother kiss his wife, not caring who was there to watch had given Claudio a strange twinge in the region of his heart.

And he was almost positive that it had impacted Therese as well. If he had not thought it impossible in the face of the night's revelations, he would have believed she was hurt that he was not that way with her. He'd seen her giving his brothers and their wives oddly wistful looks over the past couple of months and wondered at them.

Had she gone looking for affection from a man who was more outwardly expressive? The thought flayed his ego and his sense of masculine confidence. To not be all that his woman needed was not a prospect any man wanted to contemplate. Yet, how could a man who had to hide his relationship with her give her public affection?

And the relationship *was* hidden very well. Until she'd asked for divorce, Claudio had been almost certain his suspicions in that direction were mere musings of a befuddled male brain. Because he'd never once seen even a hint of impropriety on his wife's part.

He'd spent the hours on the plane going back over the last year, trying to see where she might have strayed. What had at first glance appeared to be a casual greeting took on different significance until he forced his overactive brain to stop dissecting his memories.

This was doing him no good and driving him crazy in the bargain. Claudio would let Hawk do his job and then he would confront the truth head-on. Like a man.

Like he had faced the prospect of his father's death…with no whining, or refusing to accept what such an event would mean for his own life. He had been taught since he was a small child that life must be faced and dealt with from the perspective of one's birthright. His carried more responsibility with it than most and those responsibilities pervaded every aspect of his life—including his marriage.

He had known for as long as he could remember that one day he would rule Isole dei Re. He had accepted that duty and all that it entailed on every step of the journey through his life. He had never rebelled against what his birthright dictated. There had been no need for him to make promises to his father that he would fulfill it should the unthinkable happen and the older man not survive surgery.

Both men were fully confident in Claudio's suitability for the job. He had been born to it and raised to know what that meant. He was a crown prince, destined to be a king. Yet, they *had* talked, as his father had told Therese they must…about political issues, family circumstances and personal matters.

His father had revealed a way of thinking that had shocked Claudio, but nothing more astonishing than the fact that the older man was still very much in love with Flavia.

All of the nonsense about the Scorsolini Curse his father told him about had been just that. Every mistress after Vincente's divorce (and apparently there had been none between the one indiscretion and when the marriage's dissolution became final) had been an attempt on his father's part to forget his love for a live woman. Not a dead one.

Oh, he had loved Claudio's mother all right, but he had fallen fast and deeply for Flavia. Too fast and too deep. It had made him feel incredibly guilty, like he was being unfaithful to his first beloved wife. Particularly when Flavia had gotten pregnant with Marcello. Before that, he had at least had the comfort of knowing his relationship with Flavia was merely a sexual one.

But then he had been forced to marry her and completely replace the first wife in his life. Intense feelings of guilt mixed with a grief he had never let himself vent in a public manner plagued Vincente the first years of his marriage. He had found it impossible to utter the necessary words of love to Flavia because he could not admit those feelings even to himself.

He had known his lack of outward affection had hurt Flavia, but he had told himself he could do nothing to mitigate that.

Yet, the feelings inside him grew until he was desperate to find a way to deny them. Finally, in a state of confused grief both for what he had lost and the state of his current marriage, he had betrayed his promise of fidelity. Flavia had found out and while she had been willing to suffer a marriage with love on only one side, she had refused to tolerate infidelity.

Proving she had not been raised to put duty above all, she had taken all three boys to her parents' home in Italy and filed for divorce. Out of shame, King Vincente Scorsolini had done nothing to prevent his wife divorcing him. He'd made up the fiction of the Scorsolini Curse to soothe his aching conscience and lacerated pride shortly after the divorce.

He had even believed it until he woke up to reality at Tomasso's wedding. They'd been walking along the beach with the children afterward. Vincente had taken a long look at the woman who had given birth to his third son as she chatted away with their grandchildren.

For some reason he still did not understand, but had confided to Claudio that he thought it might have been a premonition of things to come, everything had fallen into place after more than two decades of idiocy. Or so he had labeled it.

Claudio did not know what to make of his father's revelations, or why the older man had made them to him. But he knew that his father had finally accepted his love for Flavia and was prepared to act on that love. If Claudio knew his father as well as he thought he did, his stepmother's days as a single woman were numbered.

Provided King Vincente survived surgery.

CHAPTER SIX

WHEN they reached the palace, Therese managed to get out of the car and walk side by side with Claudio all the way to their private apartments without so much as making a second's eye contact or allowing her hand to brush against his. It bothered him. He did not like being ignored by his wife and she still was his wife, no matter if she wanted to pretend otherwise.

He followed her slender form into the apartment, a sense of being ill-used riding him with the tenacity of a jockey in the last leg of the Melbourne Cup.

She looked so damn lost though and it infuriated him that even amidst his own turmoil, he cared. "You should have come back to the palace with Tomasso and Maggie."

"I didn't want to," she said in that soft voice that even now impacted his libido. Damn it, she was everything he had ever wanted in a woman…except faithful.

But had she been unfaithful? Was she only thinking about it? Was her request for a divorce in preparation to entering another relationship? The questions blindsided him with the possibility that while her heart might have strayed, her body might yet remain his alone.

"I noticed," he ground out, frustrated by her on more than one level and several he did not want to examine too closely.

"I wanted to be there if anything else happened," she said with a sigh as she slipped her shoes off and padded across the sitting room in stocking feet.

The longer she went without looking at him, the more irritated he became. The fact that he found himself following her like a puppy dog did not improve his temper any, either. "You being there could have made no difference."

"That isn't what you said when we were in New York."

"I was angry."

"And taking it out on me. I noticed."

And who did she think he should have taken his anger, spawned by her request for a divorce, out on? Rather than ask a question for which he did not want an answer, he said, "I do not like the idea of you sleeping on a sofa in the waiting room. You were so out of it, you did not even notice me coming into the room."

She'd cuddled into his suit jacket, though, whispering his name as she did so and he'd felt like someone had kicked him in the gut. How could she still seek his comfort in the night when she wanted someone else?

They were in the bedroom now and she went to the cupboard to pull out a nightgown. "Security was on duty the entire time."

His tie was already long gone, but he shrugged out of the suit jacket that carried her scent mingled with his own. Like their bodies did after making love. He did not like remembering that. For reasons he could not fathom, he wanted her now more than ever.

He should be disgusted by the thought of touching her. But far from it, since considering the alternative that she was still his alone in a physical sense, the need to stamp that possession on her body once again grew with every breath he drew in. "That is not the point."

"There is no point…not to arguing about it now." She headed for the bathroom, clearly intent on finishing her changing in there when only days ago, she would have undressed in front of him quite naturally. "What is done is done."

He supposed that was how she saw the demise of their relationship, but he was not so accepting. "We agreed that we would present a united front for the time being."

"A united front does not mean I am going to start taking orders like your pet dog."

"Look at me, damn it!" he exploded, having had his fill of talking to the back or top of her head.

She did, her body turning rigidly to face him, her head coming up and her exotic green gaze glaring defiantly at him.

He glared right back, his patience completely gone. "I have never treated you in such a demeaning fashion."

"Let's not get into how you treated me at all," she said scathingly. "It doesn't matter anymore."

"Are you saying that your request for a divorce is because you are unhappy with your treatment in this marriage?" The thought had never occurred to him. The weak sense of hope that coursed through him at the possibility made him angry and yet elated at the same time.

But wouldn't a woman complain about things that bothered her before doing something as drastic as ask for a divorce? Particularly a woman as conscious of her duty as Therese?

"I did not ask for a divorce because I wanted out of our marriage over the way you treated me. If you will recall, I did not ask for a divorce at all."

"Do no argue semantics with me," he growled. "You said we had to divorce."

"We do."

"But not over my treatment of you?"

"No."

Only one circumstance could have prompted a woman as responsible and loyal as Therese to dismiss those considerations and ask for divorce. She *had* to be in love with another man. Love made fools of even the wisest and most strong minded people. Look at his own father. His love for Flavia, coming as it did when he was still in love with his dead wife, had tormented him and ultimately because of it, he had betrayed himself and her.

The thought of Therese loving another man like that evoked a feeling of jealous rage so strong it almost overcame him. He forced it down however, unwilling to give way to such weakness. "I would appreciate you having a formal pregnancy test done."

"That won't be necessary."

"Having a period is no guarantee you are not pregnant."

"And if I was pregnant…would you be bored with me? Would you still be so content to give me a divorce?" she asked with a scathing sarcasm that was entirely unlike her.

Pride forbade him give her an honest answer, so he said nothing at all.

She sighed, deflating like a pricked balloon. "That is what I thought. I'm sure I am not pregnant. Let's just leave it at that."

"You have been doing something to prevent conception?" he asked suspiciously.

How deeply had her subterfuge gone?

"*No.*"

"Then the risk is there. You will have a formal test done."

She shrugged tiredly, giving in with her body language before saying the words. "If that is what you want."

"What I want has little to do with this conversation."

"Well, it certainly isn't about what *I* want."

Claudio's expression said he thought their conversation was about exactly that. He grabbed Therese's shoulders, his grip not hurting her physically but causing mental anguish he would not begin to understand. "If you carry my child, there will be no divorce."

Which was exactly what she had thought. She didn't understand how she could feel more pain on top of everything else inside her, but she did. He'd spelled it out with words that could have no other interpretation. She mattered to him only in her capacity as potential incubator for the Scorsolini heir. For his child, he would remain married to a woman who bored him.

"Whatever you say." She was so tired and disheartened, she didn't have the energy or the desire to argue.

Besides, it didn't matter. She knew she wasn't pregnant. Having the test would not change anything.

His big body vibrated with a tension she did not understand. "You must be very certain it is not a possibility because the prospect of losing your possible freedom does not appear to upset you."

Beyond caring what she revealed, she sighed. "Perhaps because I am not overly concerned about it."

"Yet you just now told me that you are taking nothing to prevent it."

"I'm not."

"If that is true, how can you be so certain?"

"I don't lie and I am certain."

"The only evidence you have that you are not is that you have started your period. That is hardly full proof."

"I haven't started."

"But you said—"

"That I'm sure I'm not pregnant," she interrupted, just wanting the conversation over so she could take a hot shower. "I know my own body and my period is coming. All the signs are there." Including the pain of the endometriosis. Though, thankfully, so far only the twinges she had had the other night.

"As I said, your period is no guarantee."

"I told you I would have the tests. I don't understand why we have to argue about it. Can't we drop this conversation now? I want to change and go to bed."

"Yes, you agreed to have the tests, but you also told me that you wanted to have my baby *very much*. I do not know what to believe. I do not understand."

And he could not let it drop until he did.

Tears that should have been impossible considering how much she had cried already, burned the back of her eyes. "I did want to have your baby."

She still did, which made her stupid as well as a complete failure in the love stakes.

"*Did*…past tense."

"What do you expect? No woman wants to learn she is pregnant by a man who is bored with her and their marriage."

At least she shouldn't, but the thought that he would not let her go if she was pregnant taunted her, making her wish for the impossible and angry at herself for doing so. Bored or not, he would never allow the mother of his child to walk away.

"I do not know what to expect from you at all any longer,

Therese. I do not understand you," he said again, his undertone one of angry bewilderment. "I thought I knew you well, but discovered I was very wrong in that assumption."

"What difference does it make? You're bored with what you do know. You said so." She spun away and rushed into the bathroom, shutting the door behind her, unwilling to let him see how much those words hurt.

She stripped and stepped into the oversize shower stall. Not because she wanted another shower after the long one she'd taken in the hotel, but because it was the one place she could safely vent her emotions. She turned on the taps and icy cold jets of water hit her from five directions.

Her mind was in such a state of turmoil, that the frigid temperatures barely registered before the water started to warm to her preset selection on the control panel by the door. Pleasantly hot water was cascading down her body when she felt another presence in the cubicle.

She turned around, her mind telling her instincts they had to be wrong, but they were not. Claudio was there just as she had known he would be.

He stood magnificently naked, the water running in rivulets down his bronze chest. "I decided not to wait on my shower."

"Get out," she gasped.

"But why should I? We've done this together many times before."

"But everything is different now."

"You are still my wife." And there was a message there she did not quite get.

"Only temporarily," she said to punish herself as much as him.

"So you have said."

"And you agreed. You said you wanted it…the divorce," she said, unable to hide her pain at that truth.

"Perhaps I spoke hastily. I am not bored with every aspect of our relationship, *cara*. Not yet."

Was that supposed to make her feel better? It didn't and neither did the look of desire hardening his features.

"You want sex?" she asked in total shock, having just worked that out.

"Why so surprised? It is something we are very good at together."

"But you said…" He'd said that her value as a partner had gone down when she started turning him down, not that he didn't want her anymore.

"I said?"

"Things that hurt me."

"And your demand for a divorce did not hurt me?" he asked.

Had it? Probably. But then why would he want sex now? Nothing made sense anymore. "I don't understand," she said, echoing his sentiments earlier.

His dark eyes narrowed. "Welcome to the club."

"You can't want me."

"Now that is where you are wrong, Therese. Very much wrong." He leaned down and kissed her with blatant seductive intent, his lips molding hers, his big hands sliding around her waist to pull her closer to his naked maleness.

She was so stunned by this turn of events that she did nothing, neither fighting him nor acquiescing.

He lifted his head, the slumberous passion in his eyes much hotter than the water pelting their bodies. "What is the matter? You were quick enough to respond only a night ago."

How could he ask something so stupid? "That was before…"

"Before you told me we had to divorce?"

"Yes. I don't think—"

His wet hand covered her mouth. "I do not want you to think. For then I must think and I do not wish to. About anything."

And she understood…or thought she did. Had she not been so tired, she would probably have anticipated this. Claudio needed comfort. His father lay in a hospital bed, his future uncertain and her strong husband would never willingly admit fear on that score. Or any other if it came to that.

The question was what was she going to do about it?

But even as she asked herself that, a realization came to her. She needed comfort, too.

He did not love her and that hurt. King Vincente's health was at risk and that hurt as well. Even if he survived his surgery, which there was every chance he would do…she would lose him along with the other Scorsolinis from her life when her marriage ended. That knowledge added pain on top of pain.

The careful little world she had built around herself in which she had people she loved, if not those who loved her in return, was crumbling.

Soon, she would be living a life entirely separate, one in which she would have to stand on the sidelines. She would have to watch from afar while the things and people she cared about existed and thrived apart from her.

Her pet projects would be taken over by someone else, the issues she thought were so important would find another spokeswoman. Her role in the political infrastructure of Isole dei Re would be filled in by someone else, doing things differently…prioritizing differently and wanting to accomplish different things.

More painful to her heart was the knowledge that her sisters-in-law would blossom in their new roles, have their babies, and more children besides. All without her around to experience, if only vicariously, the reality of a family love.

Flavia and Vincente would finally find their way back to each other…it was obvious to anyone with eyes in her head that they were head over heels in love and always had been. But she would not be around to rejoice with them. She would once again be on the outside looking in.

She would try to fill her life with meaningful endeavors, but the cold winds of loneliness were already blowing across her soul. Because most devastating of all, Claudio would one day remarry and have his own children and they would not be hers.

Pain so intense it was physical shook her frame as Claudio stared down into her eyes, his own expression unreadable except for the physical need that burned in his dark gaze. "I want you, *cara.* If you are honest with yourself…you will admit you want me, too."

She looked down where his gaze had traveled. Her breasts were flushed a soft pink with desire, her nipples as hard and crimson as frozen berries. They ached under his hot scrutiny, the skin tight and throbbing with the blood pulsing below it and the engorged tips crying out for the relief of his touch.

A million memories of how it felt to have his mouth and his hands on her erogenous zones tormented her mind. And what he could not see, but she could feel, was the way her most intimate flesh had swollen as well and throbbed with a need to be filled by him, connected to him.

Both her emotional pain and the physical need surging through her sprang from the deep well of love she had for him. It did not matter that he did not return that love. It was too much a part of her being to dismiss and each set of emotions caused by her love warred for supremacy.

One promised empty loneliness that tears would not assuage and the other oblivion. She chose the oblivion. "Yes, I want you," she said with some despair.

He took no further urging, but swooped down on her mouth with the speed and power of an invading armada as he yanked her into full-body contact. His lips devoured hers and his hard, masculine body imprinted a message of sexual need on her own.

It was one that found an answering craving in her and she did not remain passive against him, but touched him as if it would be the last time. She reveled in the contrast her fingertips found between the silky tautness of his skin and the whorls of dark curling hair that marked his body so different from her own. A man's body, the epitome of masculine perfection to her senses.

She traced the outlines of ridges created by honed muscle, memorizing anew the way his body felt. She did not know how she was going to live the rest of her life without this. It was too special…so perfect, she often cried afterward at the sheer beauty of the feelings he evoked in her.

Tears burned her eyes and she blinked them away as the hot water masked any signs of her inner turmoil. Her hand hovered above his hardness, her nails scoring through the nest of dark hair from which it sprang. His big body trembled and sounds of need rumbled from deep in his chest.

Incredible how much she loved those sounds. She was addicted to them and she had spent hours in bed with him listening, watching, paying oh so very close attention to his reactions so she could have more…and more…and more.

His hands were busy, too, molding her breasts and caressing sensitive areas he knew so well. It was as if he knew this was a special moment in time, a unique opportunity that might not come again because he touched her so carefully, arousing her to a fever pitch of sensation. And she made her own sounds of desire, moans and whimpers that mixed with the beat of the pouring water.

Her control slipped moment by moment until she was a living, breathing, quivering mass of feminine sexual need. She cried out against his lips from his touch even as she demanded more with the movement of her body and hungrily caressed his body with all the fire burning inside her.

The sound of Therese's sexy whimpers drove Claudio crazy as she went wild for him. She had always been incredibly responsive…when she let him touch her, but there was a quality to her response right now that had never been there before. Her body shook and trembled and her hands were all over him, so hot against his skin that he felt singed.

She touched him with a furious desperation. As if she had never touched him before…*or would never touch him again*.

But he dismissed that last thought as ludicrous in the face of how much she so obviously wanted him. This kind of desire did not get assuaged in one attempt at lovemaking… or even a hundred. He should know. He wanted her that much.

Would always want her.

And his shy and proper wife was practically climbing his body in an attempt to join her body with his. She was completely out of control and he refused to believe she could give even a fraction of this reaction to another man.

She might think she wanted someone else for reasons he had yet to discover, but it was he who could touch the very core of her soul with a simple hand to her breast.

It had been that way since the very first time he touched her with the intent to seduce.

Their sexual connection was too strong to be tampered with, too primitive to be explained or even understood on an intellectual level. She might have withheld herself from him more in the past few months than she had at first, but when she did allow him close…she went to pieces. Perhaps not as spectacularly as this time, but definitely too strongly for him to seriously believe she could want another man.

No way could she be this way with anyone else and still respond in such a primal fashion to him…not his wife, a woman who had spent her whole life tamping down her emotional reactions and hiding them. It went against everything he knew her to be.

Unless she was thinking of the other man when Claudio touched her…unless she was using him to assuage a need she could not have met another way.

Where the thought came from, he did not know, but it detonated with the power of a nuclear blast in his head. *No, damn it. He would not believe that.* And yet, it made sense of a woman who asked for a divorce and then made love like she would die if she could not have his touch.

He broke his mouth from hers as he lifted her up his body to position his hardness at the entrance to her slickened flesh. He had to have her…even the disturbing thoughts could not dampen his need, but he couldn't allow her to use him like that. He would not let that scenario be reality for them. *"Say my name…ask me to take you."*

Her eyes opened, revealing beautiful green and very dazed depths. "Wh-what?"

"Who am I?" he ground out in harsh demand.

"Amore mio."

The words slammed through him like a sledgehammer…was that her pet name for the other man or was she calling Claudio her love? He could count on one hand the number of times she had used that expression with him during their marriage and none of them in the last six months. "My *name,* say it."

Her lips curved softly, her expression an odd mixture he could not decipher. It seemed as if both exultation and sadness resided in her green gaze, but that made no sense. "Claudio…my prince."

Then she leaned forward to reconnect their lips and kissed him with desperate passion, devouring his mouth before kissing along his jaw until she was right at his ear. She whispered, "Love me, Claudio. Please. Be one with me…if only for a little while."

Her voice had a strange quality to it, as if it was not merely sex she was asking for, but he did not know what else she wanted. He could give her the sex, though. Was in fact dying to do so. He levered her body onto his shaft at the same time as surging upward so that he was impaled in one urgent thrust.

She cried out, her head falling back on her shoulders, her expression one of agonized bliss.

He grunted, a sound that was entirely primitive and would have at any other time embarrassed his sophisticated sense of self. "You feel so good around me, *amante.*"

"You feel…perfect…inside…me…" she gasped out as he withdrew and thrust again.

Therese thought maybe she would die from pleasure. If she did, it would be the way to go...so much better than the pain inflicted by the endometriosis every month.

The feel of him inside of her was so incredible. She and Claudio had made love many times in many ways, but never anything as primal and basic as this. There was no bed to support them. He was not even using the wall to support her as he had other times they had made love in the shower, just sheer animal strength.

It was as if they were in a world entirely apart from anything normal, anything they had known before. Steam surrounded them like a heated fog as hot water cascaded down their bodies locked in ecstatic intimacy.

She cried out as he thrust upward and hit that special pleasure zone inside her.

"That is right, *mi moglie*. Come apart for me. Show me this side to you that no one else ever sees." His mouth landed on her neck, sucking, nibbling, licking and sending shivers of sensation to the most sensitive areas of her body.

She locked her ankles behind his back and rode him... he surged into her...she squeezed his hardness into her... he guided her body with a bruising grip on her hips and buttocks.

She opened her eyes to look at him and saw that his head was thrown back in abandon like hers had been, his face etched with sexual pleasure. She leaned forward and bit his chest in an act so primitive, even in her advanced state of passion...it shocked her.

He was not shocked, though, but merely growled and increased the rhythm, slamming into her with pounding force with every thrust. It was so intense, she felt like she was on the verge of shattering into a million over-pleasured bits.

Tension spiraled inside her, a feeling of leaping from one experience to the next up a circular incline, traveling toward a precipice and then going over as her body convulsed around him and she cried out his name. She was falling too fast and she cried out in fright.

He gripped her tighter and she wrapped her arms around him, pressing to his body, the only sense of reality in a universe exploding from pleasure. He was silent when he climaxed, his teeth bared in a feral grimace that said more eloquently than any words could have how intensely he was feeling.

CHAPTER SEVEN

AFTERWARD, he wrapped her up against him, soothing her with gentle words and tender caresses against her back until the sobs she had not realized she was crying ebbed. Her body relaxed slowly, until she dangled in his arms, a boneless heap.

He held her for several long and silent moments, while her legs dangled and the connection between their bodies remained, reminding her that once was rarely enough for this man...even when their lovemaking culminated in a mind-blowing pleasure that left her completely spent.

Finally he lifted her off of him and began washing her with gentle hands that touched every inch of her as if to say, "Mine. Mine. And this is mine, too."

She tried to return the favor, but her hands were clumsy, her movements jerky with a special kind of fatigue only he could induce. Eventually he turned off the water and stepped out of the shower, his arm still supporting her.

She forced herself to move away so they could dry off, but even in that he ended up helping her. Then he pulled her into his body and walked her from the bathroom, her nightgown forgotten on the floor of the en suite.

They climbed into bed together and she went willingly

into his arms, closing her eyes, so tired that she fell asleep immediately.

She woke scant hours later to a kiss on her temple. "Wake up, *cara*. We must hurry and dress or we will not make it to the hospital before they take Papa down to surgery."

She sat up, feeling out of sorts. Despite the pleasure of lovemaking beforehand, she had had disturbing dreams and her sleep had not been restful. Pain was dragging at her lower abdomen and she wished she could have kept on sleeping. Because restful, or not, it was at least a respite from the reality she was loathe to face.

Her period was due soon, not that it was super regular now that she wasn't on the pill. But she knew the pain would only get worse every day until it started and unbearable during the flow of blood from her body.

Claudio was already half dressed and looked over his shoulder as he did his tie. "Get a move on, Therese."

She nodded, wincing as her head ached from the movement. She climbed gingerly from bed, her eyes glued to his figure. That at least gave pleasure. She could not imagine life without this man and said so before she thought better of the admission.

He stopped in the act of pulling on his suit coat. "But you do not have to. After last night, it is obvious we can forget this talk of divorce."

"Are you saying you aren't bored with me anymore?"

"You need to ask after our sojourn in the shower?" he asked with the devil's own smile.

But she did not smile in return. Their time in the shower had been incredible, but they had spent what remained of the night wrapped in each other's arms. Only he didn't mention that, did he?

Sex. That was all he wanted from her and when it was on offer, she was the perfect wife. He'd said that when he told her he was bored with her…that her value had dropped significantly when she began turning him down. The fact that the night before and his reaction to it only supported that truth was not a particularly pleasant reality.

She turned her head away. "Last night did not change anything important."

He said a truly foul word and her gaze flew back to him.

He finished shrugging into his coat, his dark brown eyes hard as granite. "You are *not* telling me you still think a divorce is necessary. I refuse to accept you are saying that."

"But that is what I am saying," she admitted wearily, her head now pounding.

The look he gave her would have brought about her demise if looks truly could have been lethal. He looked like he hated her and he didn't say another single, solitary word. He simply finished dressing and left their room.

Moving as quickly as she could with the cramps now reaching toward debilitating levels, she dressed as well and followed him. She found him downstairs, giving instructions to his father's assistant as well as his own.

"The others are waiting for us in the car," he said when he saw her. Then he dismissed the employees and headed toward the back of the palace where the car would be parked.

"Claudio."

"Do not speak to me, Therese." The venom in his voice silenced her as effectively as a gag.

He did hate her.

He was like that for the rest of the morning, only managing to maintain a thin veil of civility in front of his family. It slipped to blatant hostility when they were not within earshot.

The one bright spot was that King Vincente came through the surgery with flying colors and was mostly lucid for visits with his family afterward. When Flavia offered to stay at the hospital with him, he gratefully accepted and sent the rest of them home with a good dose of his trademark arrogance.

Despite her father-in-law's continuing improvement in health, the next few days were a torment for Therese. Both in mind and body. Claudio stayed in their suite for appearance's sake, but the width of the Great Divide ran down the middle of their bed…that was when he was in it. He also refused to speak to her when they were alone, except to discuss their respective duties.

If she even looked like she was going to get personal, he made an excuse to leave…or walked away without an excuse. When he was there to begin with. Which wasn't often. She saw him more frequently in the company of others than she did in the privacy of their suite and that was rare enough.

He had always had a backbreaking schedule, but now it was even worse. He had to cover both his own responsibilities and those of his father. As a world leader, those duties were such that he could not leave any of them undone. He'd always functioned on less sleep than she did, but now she wondered sometimes if he slept at all.

His brothers pitched in where they could, but Claudio's role in the family dictated that the majority of the decisions, responsibility and stress fell squarely on his broad shoulders.

No matter how much his angry rejection hurt, she felt badly for him, worried about him and wished about ten times a day that she had waited to ask for a divorce until after the crisis had passed. He refused to accept comfort or help from her in any form and she didn't blame him, but she longed to help him somehow.

Her request for a divorce had stung his pride and shattered his ego when he could least afford that kind of wounding. He needed a full store of inner strength in his current circumstance, but he was handicapped by his anger over her defection. She wanted to explain that it wasn't defection, but the physical pain from her endometriosis and the haziness resultant from the drugs she took to control it depleted her ability to pursue anything.

It was all she could do to make it through each day, much less fight with her husband to put their marriage to rights…only to convince him that it had to end anyway.

In every way she looked, she couldn't help but see that it would have been so much easier on both her and Claudio if she had waited to tell him of their need to divorce until after he got back from his trip to New York. At least then, all of this hostility and energy draining anger during such a critical time could have been avoided.

The guilt of hindsight weighed her down, making it harder than usual to deal with her physical pain and there were some nights she simply laid in her lonely bed and cried. As the doctor had predicted, this month's pain was worse than the one before once her period arrived and some days she didn't know how she was going to survive it.

Her own duties did not magically disappear because of the family crisis, but in fact increased. And she had to spend at least part of every day at the hospital, where she put on her best front. She visited King Vincente and made sure Flavia was not wearing herself out playing nursemaid and then would go home only to worry about Claudio.

She was leaving King Vincente's room one evening when she ran into Claudio.

He looked almost haggard with tiredness, but when he saw her, the mask of invincibility fell into place.

"You need to rest," she said instead of a greeting, laying her hand on his arm.

He shrugged off her touch with a frown. "I am fine."

"No, you aren't. Everyone says you're pushing yourself too hard, but no one knows what to do about it."

"There is nothing to do. It is my duty to care for my country while my father is ill."

"Your brothers—"

"Have their own responsibilities."

"They're worried about you."

He glared down at her. "Did one of them ask you to speak to me?"

"Yes," she said with a sigh. "Both of them actually."

"I should have known you would not evince concern on your own."

"I care about you, Claudio."

"Of a certainty…you do not."

She winced at the surety of his tone and the cynicism in his dark gaze. "I'm sorry."

"So am I. Now if you will excuse me, I have only twenty-five minutes to spend with my father."

"Are you coming home afterward?"

"No."

"You have to sleep sometime."

"Is that an invitation to your bed?"

Without volition, her expression twisted in revulsion at the thought of sharing her body intimately with him while pain racked her so incessantly.

He paled, his gaze hardening. "Well, that says it all, does it not?"

"No." She reached out to grab him before he could walk away. "Please, Claudio, listen to me."

He glared down at her. "You have nothing to say that I would want to hear."

A cramp so severe sliced through her she slumped against the wall the moment it hit her. She couldn't do this right now. Casualties were all around her and she could do nothing to help any of them. Her own self included.

"All right. I'll see you later…whenever." Forcing limbs to walk that just wanted to crumble, she left.

Claudio watched Therese leave with a mixture of rage and incomprehension. She behaved as if his cold attitude really hurt her, but she was the one who wanted a divorce. When she'd told him she still wanted it even after their incredible lovemaking, he'd been gutted.

She had just been using him.

The knowledge had hurt more than anything he had ever known, which in turn had filled him with fury. She wasn't supposed to hurt him. She was his woman, flesh of his flesh…bone of his bone. The quintessential helpmate and lover…only she'd turned out to be a betrayer instead.

The fury brought about by that realization had not abated in six days. He walked around feeling like a bomb ready to explode. He was grateful for the extra workload of his father's responsibilities because it gave him an outlet for the energy generated by his suppressed emotions.

He did not want his brothers to worry, but he had no intention of slowing down.

His father and his country needed him even if his wife did not.

* * *

Therese woke late that night to horrific pain and the sensation of sticky wetness on her thighs.

She'd bled through.

It wasn't anything new since the endometriosis had begun, but usually if she got up and changed frequently in the night, she didn't have to worry about it. She'd been so exhausted when she went to bed that she slept four hours straight.

She'd also forgotten to take her pain meds, she now remembered.

She tried to get up to take care of both problems, but fell back to the bed, a cry of pain tearing from her throat. The tiniest movement brought about sheer agony.

But remaining still hurt, too. So much she could barely breathe because of it.

She looked across the empty expanse of the bed. Claudio was not there of course. He often did not come to bed until the wee hours of the morning, if he came to bed at all. He'd slept in his office on a couple of nights and no one but she was the wiser. After their altercation at the hospital, he would no doubt be planning to do that again tonight.

Pain tore through her and she moaned, tears drenching her eyes and wetting her cheeks hotly as her body contorted in misery. If she could just get to the pain meds, but she couldn't even reach the bedside table.

How could she have forgotten to take them?

She inched toward the edge of the bed, but the progress was slow going. How far away was the table? Pain made everything around her hazy. Maybe if she rolled. She pushed from one side to her stomach and almost blacked out from the pain. It would have been welcome if she had, she thought muzzily.

Still feeling dizzy, she pushed to her back to complete

the roll, but instead of coming down on the mattress, she felt nothing but air and then landed on the floor with a thump. She could hear someone whimpering and she wanted to help them, but she couldn't move. She tried to focus in the near darkness, but could barely make out the shape of her nightstand. It looked further away than it had from the bed.

She reached for it, sobs wrenching from her throat and doing nothing to lessen the pain racking her body.

"Therese? What the hell is going on?" The overhead light came on, turning everything from black and white to glaring Technicolor.

It hurt her eyes and she closed them, collapsing against the floor in a shivering heap as Claudio cursed in voluble Italian.

"What happened?" He dropped to her side, his hand on her shoulder. "You are bleeding. I will call an ambulance."

"No!" She looked up at her tall, gorgeous husband, her eyes awash with tears she was trying to blink back now that he was here to see them. "I need my pain pills. In… the…drawer," she gasped out around another wave of cramping.

"Pain meds are not going to stop this bleeding."

"Don't need to…it's my period."

"Like hell. You are hemorrhaging."

He picked up the phone and she cried out. "No! *Please, Claudio*…" she gasped and then moaned as pain snaked through her. "Just get me…" She panted, trying to get enough breath to go on. "The bed. Please. Hurts…" She curled into a fetal position.

He dropped the phone and then she felt a blanket settling over her. He tucked it around her as he picked her up, but he did not lay her on the bed. He headed for the door.

"Where…going?" she asked weakly.

"The hospital and you can save your arguments. I won't call an ambulance if that's what you want, but you need a doctor."

"I've seen a doctor. Told you…my pills…*need them*."

"You need a hell of a lot more than pain pills," he ground out without breaking his stride.

"Yes. Surgery. Not today."

"Yes, today. If that is what you need, you get it now."

"Can't."

"Why not?" he asked as he stopped in front of the intercom by their door.

"Not safe." She looked at him, her face contorting with another spasm of pain. "Please. I need the pills."

He looked down at her, his eyes narrowed. "You need a doctor."

"Please," she begged, in so much pain she would have given anything for those pills.

His jaw looked hewn from rock. "All right, but you had better be right about the blood. I will not let you die on me. Do you hear?"

He jogged back into the bedroom, careful not to jar her and then he gently laid her onto the bed before opening the bedside drawer. He pulled out a prescription bottle, looked at it and then opened it, shaking two tablets into his hand. There was a glass of water beside the bed.

She'd poured it from the carafe and put it there to take her pills with and then spaced it, she now remembered. One of the negative side effects of taking them to begin with was her spotty memory. She lived in fear of taking too many and overdosing, which might explain the number of times she ended up in severe pain wishing she'd kept to her schedule.

He put his arm behind her shoulder and lifted her into a semisitting position and helped her take the pills as if she could not do it herself. And the truth was, she couldn't. It was taking everything she had not to scream at the agony ripping through her insides.

After she swallowed the pills, he carefully laid her back on the bed.

"How long?"

"Twenty to thirty minutes."

"Can I do anything else?"

She was in far too much pain to refine on the fact that the man asking had been treating her like a leper for the last few days. "Hot water helps."

"To drink or to soak in?"

"Soaking...shower, too."

He nodded and disappeared into the bathroom. She heard water running and then he was back and he was naked. She couldn't make sense of that and didn't even try.

She simply tried to control the pain as he picked up the phone beside the bed and spoke some instructions into it about having the bed cleaned and remade. She was just glad he wasn't calling a doctor in after all.

She had gone through too much to keep her secret from the media...she didn't want to risk it with a doctor. Even a Scorsolini Royals approved one.

"I am going to undress you."

"Okay," she said woozily, the drugs taking effect quickly because she'd taken them without food.

He removed the blanket and her clothes with careful hands. He cursed when he saw how much blood was on her legs. He surveyed her grimly. "You are certain this is only period blood?"

"Yes."

He shook his head, but didn't say anything. He simply bent and lifted her from the bed. As gentle as he was, the movement still jarred her and brought on a wave of dizziness as pain overcame her again.

She moaned.

He cursed. "This cannot be normal, *cara.*"

"Didn't say it was normal," she muttered, her eyes shut, her head lolling against his shoulder.

Strangely he didn't ask what it was.

"I'm surprised," she said.

"About?"

"You aren't demanding answers."

"You do not have any idea how terrible you look, do you?"

"I look terrible?" she asked, a fresh spate of tears rolling down her cheeks. "Ugly?"

"Ill, you foolish woman. You are as white as paper and you look like even a weak wind would blow you over."

"I hurt."

"I know." And he sounded like the knowledge was tearing him apart, but that had to be a trick of her hearing.

Why would he care if she hurt when he hated her?

Only the way he held her was not the cruel grip of hatred or even the impersonal grip of a stranger. He held her to him like she was precious in some way and even if it was a delusion, she clung to him, needing the comfort and too weak to pretend otherwise.

She didn't realize where they were headed until he stepped into the already steaming shower with her and then she understood why he'd gotten naked, too. He planned to hold her while she bathed. Tears of relief seeped from beneath her closed eyelids as the hot water cascaded over her skin.

He hadn't left her alone to face her pain and she felt pathetically grateful. She kept her eyes closed, not caring that some sprayed her face. He directed water over her legs, balancing her on his knee so he could wash the blood away.

"There's so much," he repeated in a subdued undertone.

"It gets worse every month," she said, wondering at her lack of embarrassment to have him caring for her like this.

But then how many times had she wished he was there to take care of her, that he cared enough to notice how hard her monthly had become and comforted her because of it? Such thoughts had always been in the realm of fantasy before, but now it was a reality and she had a hard time taking it in.

He took care of her with an efficiency and instinctual understanding she couldn't help but admire.

She didn't know how long they showered, but at some point he said, "I think you're safe for the whirlpool now. The bleeding has either stopped or slowed down considerably."

"It comes in fits and starts," she said tiredly as she let him carry her dripping wet to the whirlpool bath.

He didn't drop her into it like she expected, but climbed the steps and stepped down into it with her still in his arms. She made a sound of protest.

"You cannot bathe by yourself in this condition."

"I only plan to lie here."

"And so you will…in my arms."

She didn't argue any further as he settled her between his legs with his arms around her torso so that she did not have to worry about staying afloat or staying put. He took care of it all for her. She sighed contentedly, the meds beginning to take effect and leaned back against him peacefully.

She should probably feel guilty for letting him take care of her like he was taking care of everyone else right now, but it felt too good…too right for guilt. *And resting in a whirlpool was not a bad thing for him, either,* a voice inside her head told her convincingly.

As the pain receded and her sense of well being increased, she let herself relax totally. "This is nice."

"Are you feeling better?"

"Yes." She sighed. "But we'll have to get out soon."

"Why?"

"I may start bleeding again."

He sighed. "We have established that this is not a normal period."

"No, it's not."

"What is going on?"

"I tried to tell you on the plane from New York, but you didn't want to hear." Which was an accusation, not an answer, but it still hurt he'd been so ready to dismiss their marriage that he hadn't even cared what her reasons were for believing it had to end.

"No. I would remember."

"Yes, I did."

"When did you try to tell me about this awful bleeding and pain?" he asked, still sounding as if he doubted her.

"When I wanted to tell you why we have to end our marriage, but then you told me you wanted it over anyway and it didn't seem to matter." Try as she might, she could not make herself treat it lightly.

It had devastated her and that remembered devastation was in her voice.

Tension filled the muscular body cradling hers so close. "This is why you asked for a divorce? Because of this pain and bleeding?"

CHAPTER EIGHT

"In a way, yes."

"Explain what way."

"I don't look terrible anymore?" she asked with some of her old sense of humor.

"You sound so tired you can barely stay awake and I should leave this until tomorrow, but I cannot."

"Neither can I," she admitted. She wanted the truth out. She wanted him to stop looking at her as if she'd sold him out to the enemy.

"I have endometriosis."

"What is that?"

She tried to wrap her muddled mind around the clinical description the doctor had given her. "It is a condition linked to my menstrual cycle."

"I had figured that much out myself."

"Yes, well…I'm not a doctor. Explaining diseases doesn't come easily to me."

"I apologize. I should not have been sarcastic."

"It's all right." She was glad he wasn't looking in her face, that their position precluded eye contact because she didn't think she could get through this if she had to see his reaction to her news.

"I…um…"

"Begin at the beginning. What causes the pain?"

"In clinical terms, it's where tissue similar to that in my uterus finds its way into other parts of my pelvic area… well, it can go other places, but isn't as likely to."

"Che cosa?" he asked, sounding shocked.

"Did you have sex education in school?"

"Isole dei Re requires a certain amount of information imparted in its public school system during the final years before university."

"And you went to public school?" she asked with interest, never having actually wondered on that point before.

She knew that his brother's children attended a public school, but Diamante was a small island. She'd never asked if the princes had done the same thing in Lo Paradiso growing up.

"*Sì*. Of course. If it is good enough for our people, it is good enough for us."

"That's not the attitude of most of the world's royalty."

"We are unique," he said, his voice loaded with arrogance.

"Definitely."

"Enough of the school system, explain this tissue you mentioned."

"Well, I was going to say, can you remember the pictures in sex ed or health class of the female reproductive system?"

"*Sì*. I am not so old my school days are a blur."

"Good. Picture little dots of tissue on the outside of the fallopian tubes, or the ovaries…or lining the vaginal walls."

The muscular thighs beneath her were rigid with tension. "You are saying you have growths in all these places?"

"Yes."

He cursed.

She sighed. "It could be worse. I'm actually lucky." But not as lucky as the women who did not have the added complication of infertility.

"You do not sound lucky. So these lesions cause pain?"

"They aren't cuts…they're growths, but they fill with blood during the menstrual cycle. There's nowhere for it to go and that causes pain. Lots of pain," she added for good measure.

"This pain…it makes it difficult to make love, no?"

She bit her lip and nodded.

"This is why you have been turning me down so much these past months?" he asked, his voice curiously neutral.

"Yes," she said on a sigh.

"I do not understand why divorce. Surely you know that if you had told me about the pain, I would not have asked for sex."

If only it were that simple. "Yes, I knew that." But knowing it did not change the fact that without the sex she had little value to him.

He might have stayed married to her without the infertility issue, but he would not have been happy about it. She wondered if she had not blundered in her telling, though, if she would ever have known that. She had the sneaking suspicion that his anger had made him more honest than he ever would have been otherwise.

"So, why divorce?"

"My doctor said that between thirty and forty percent of the women who have endometriosis become infertile."

He sucked in a charged breath and then let it out. "Which means that sixty to seventy percent do not."

"I am not one of them."

"What are you saying?"

"The doctor told me that there was almost no chance I could conceive without IVF and even then, there could be no guarantees."

"But you were tested for infertility before our marriage."

"Endometriosis isn't something you can predict. They aren't even sure of what causes it. There are no markers that would show up on tests before it begins happening, so the doctors had no way of knowing that I would have it, much less the impact it would have on my ability to conceive."

"And your doctor, he is certain of the impact it has had on your reproductive capabilities?"

"Yes."

He was silent and she could not stand that silence, so she said, "There are some researchers who estimate it is the cause of up to fifty percent of female infertility."

Which said nothing about the emotional devastation that all too significant statistic wrought. Cold numbers were only that until applied to a flesh and blood woman whose life was forever altered by the disease.

"Obviously many women have this condition then."

"Yes." She could have given him numbers, but they didn't matter. The fact that millions of other women suffered from it did not alter her circumstances.

She was defective and as much as she wished it otherwise, that could not be changed.

"When did it start?"

"I'm not sure. My doctor said that birth control pills are one of the prescribed therapies. It could have started any time since our marriage…even before, but I didn't know because I didn't think the monthly cramps I had were all that unusual."

"The tests…"

"I told you, there is no test for it that gives a marker. Routine fertility tests would only have told us whether my system had been affected prior to our marriage and it wasn't."

"So, you could have had it all along?"

"Yes, but it doesn't usually hit until a woman is in her mid-twenties."

"I see."

"Do you?" She wished she did.

"How did you discover you were suffering from it now?"

"The pain."

"I am sorry."

"Me, too. After I went off the pill, I started bleeding more and hurting way more than I used to during my monthly."

"You never said anything."

"It wasn't your burden to carry."

"How can you say that? I am your husband."

"But I am responsible for myself."

"So you took it upon yourself to find out what was wrong?"

"Not at first, but…" She sighed and told him about the time she woke from a faint with blood beneath her on the bathroom floor. "After that, I knew I had to find out what was wrong."

"Even then, you kept it to yourself."

"It's the way I was raised."

"I cannot believe your parents would have expected you to deal with something of this magnitude on your own."

"Then you do not know them as well as you think you do." Suddenly overcome with tiredness, she slumped back against him.

The pain bombs were having their predictable effect and

her brain was turning to mush. Thankfully she had said pretty much everything that needed saying.

"Perhaps," he admitted, surprising her. Normally he was too arrogant to admit the possibility he was wrong. "You have had the diagnosis confirmed absolutely?"

"Yes." She turned her head against him and closed her eyes, her body so relaxed, she was close to sleep.

He said something, but she didn't quite comprehend it. "Therese…"

"Hmm…"

"You are not tracking."

"The pills make me loopy. I want to go to sleep now."

She didn't have to tell him twice. He lifted her out of the tub and took care of her as if she were a small child. He dried her and dressed her, making sure she was prepared for more nocturnal bleeding.

Then he carried her through to the bedroom and laid her down on a miraculously clean bed. "The blankets don't have blood anymore."

"I instructed the staff to change it while we were in the bath."

"Oh."

"You did not hear me?"

"Don't know…I miss a lot of stuff when I'm on the pain pills." But vaguely she remembered that phone call. She opened her mouth to tell him so, but then closed it again when she forgot what she was going to say.

"I see."

"What?" she asked muzzily, wondering what he could see that he thought he needed to make note of.

Strange man, her husband.

He said something that she didn't answer. She was too

busy snuggling into her pillow and falling asleep. She vaguely registered being taken into his arms before slipping into total oblivion.

Claudio stared down at the detective's report on his desk with unseeing eyes. It held no great revelations. Not after last night. He now knew…everything. There was no other man. Therese had not been unfaithful, nor did she want to divorce him because she wanted to move on to something better.

She had a medical condition that apparently affected at least one in ten women between the ages of twenty-five and forty. He could not imagine it, had never heard of it and in some respects that made him angry. One day he would be sovereign of his country…did he not need to know about things like this?

Perhaps he and the minister of health should discuss the compilation of a report of women's health issues. He was a twenty-first century prince…not a patriarch from an outmoded era. He was sure his father would agree.

So would Therese…or she would have before. In fact, she would have insisted on taking the project over…before. Now she was intent on leaving him. Filing for divorce and ending their marriage—all because this strange disease had left her virtually infertile.

She saw no hope for their future, but his entire being rebelled at such a solution to her predicament.

He would not let her go.

Only he had this awful suspicion that it wasn't going to be about what *he* wanted. Therese could be incredibly stubborn and she had decided that their marriage was no longer viable because she could not guarantee giving him children—an heir to his throne. Even if he could convince her that he did not see things that way, that he wanted her to stay, she might insist on leaving for the good of Isole dei Re.

She took her duty to her adopted country seriously. She had spent several months hiding debilitating pain and excessive bleeding in order to protect its inhabitants and the rest of the royal family from turmoil and speculation over her health. He could not believe he had been stupid enough now to believe that she would have an affair.

Even if she fell in love, she was too intensely aware of her duty to ever do anything to compromise her position. Which knowledge did not make him feel better, though it should have.

Not when she had refused to discuss anything further that morning. She had insisted she had no time if she was going to visit his father before her other duties began for the day. And she had laughed sarcastically when he had suggested that perhaps she should stay in bed and rest.

She'd curled her lip at him with a most un-Therese-like expression. "I've been dealing with this for months now and I'm not in the habit of abandoning my responsibilities because of it."

"But you are ill." And he had not known it, damn it.

"I was ill last month, too, but I did not take to my bed."

"Perhaps you should have."

"This from the man who read me the riot act for canceling my appointments to fly to New York to see him?"

His reaction to that event was going to haunt him for a long time, he just knew it. "I did not realize what was at stake at the time."

"*Nothing* was at stake."

"You can say that when you asked for a divorce?"

"I can say that when I know it to be true. The timing of

my telling you was unfortunate. I should have waited to tell you about my condition until you got back."

"No, you should have told me about your condition as you call it as soon as it began happening." And definitely before she had asked for a divorce, but he wasn't about to say that.

Blaming his vicious reaction to what he thought was news of an affair on her would not help the situation at all. He had to pay for his sins with humility…though it would not be easy to do. It was not a natural state of mind for him.

"You weren't around to tell," she said with unexpected anger, her green eyes snapping at him with derision. "Not during that time of month. You were always careful to plan your out of town business trips for when I wasn't available sexually."

She made it sound like she'd been nothing more than a sexual convenience. "It was not like that."

"It was and is exactly like that. You've been doing it since practically the beginning of our marriage."

"But it is not because I saw you as only a sexual convenience." He'd begun scheduling his trips that way when he realized it embarrassed Therese for him to make sexual overtures during her menses. He always wanted her, so the best solution was to get out of temptation's path.

"You could have fooled me."

"Apparently, I did."

She shrugged. "I have to go."

But he could not leave it there. "I was not *always* gone during your periods. You could have told me, but you chose to hide it from me instead."

"You didn't make it very hard, did you?"

"What the hell is that supposed to mean?"

"You've been swearing a lot lately," she said with what he thought was total irrelevance.

"And you have been lying to me for months."

"Covering…it's not the same thing. Ask any politician."

"But you are not a politician. You are my wife."

She pulled on a short pink-and-brown tweed jacket that matched her stylish skirt and flipped her hair out from her collar. "I am a princess…in today's age, that makes me a politician."

"It is because you are my wife that you are a princess. Our relationship comes first."

"Like it did in New York?" she asked as she headed for the door.

"You took me by surprise."

She opened the door, her expression one of cool challenge. "Hindsight is always twenty-twenty, or so they say, but your eyesight has been purely myopic where I'm concerned from the very beginning, Claudio. You see what you want to see, perceive only what is convenient and totally disregard everything else. Trying to rewrite our short history for the sake of my feelings or your pride will not change that reality."

"I thought you were happy being my wife." At least he had until the last few months.

"I was, but that doesn't alter the fact that you made it so easy to hide my illness from you. Why was it so easy, Claudio? Why didn't you care enough to notice that some months it was all I could do to hold it together?"

He had no answer, his gut tightening at the question and something in the region of his heart squeezing in a painful vise. She had turned and walked away then. No more questions. No histrionics, just a dignified exit…something she excelled at.

He had made it a point to be at the palace for lunch, but she had treated him like he was a stranger. Tomasso, Maggie and Flavia had been there as well and he had received a few odd looks from each of them, but no one pried. Flavia had looked at Therese several times, her brown gaze darkened with worry…but still no questions were asked.

And Claudio wondered why it was that an obvious problem could exist and yet no one remark upon it, but he could never remember it being any different. They were a royal family and they did not air their concerns in public, but when had that stretched to meaning he should not ask his wife why the heck she was acting so loopy?

He'd made assumptions about what that had meant and could not have been more off target if he had tried. He had believed she was having an affair and it had gutted him. But never once had he simply asked why she did not want to make love as frequently, why she zoned off when they were talking sometimes and why she had started pulling away from him.

Why hadn't he?

The easy answer was that he had not wanted to hear what he thought was the answer, but it was more complicated than that. It had to do with an unspoken rule in his family that one did not discuss unpleasantness. A rule he had been completely unaware of on a conscious level until now.

The Scorsolinis were men of action, but talking about something as esoterical as feelings was an anathema to most of them. And admitting weakness was even worse. To have admitted he was worried, that he missed her formerly generous passion in bed would have been beyond his ability.

Which meant what? That he was willing to pretend nothing had changed when things patently had changed for the sake of his pride.

While all along, his wife had been battling this horrible, painful disease and telling no one. Because no one had asked. *He had not asked.* Guilt consumed him. He should have known something was wrong, even without asking. She was right…he'd made it too easy for her to hide her illness, but not because he had not cared.

Would he be able to convince her of that?

He got the impression she did not think he cared at all and nothing could be further from the truth. He had thought she was growing bored with his lovemaking when in fact she had simply been protecting herself. Did she not realize that a man needed to know these things?

Looking down at the report he had to acknowledge that there apparently was a great deal she had kept from him during their three-year marriage. Things she had obviously not realized he needed to know.

He found it incomprehensible that she had a secret doctor in Miami who had diagnosed her. She'd said that she had been going to this doctor for anything of a delicate nature since the very beginning of their marriage. How many appointments had she kept in secret, how many trips had she made and worked the visit in?

And how had she managed to do it while traveling with a security detail? He did not like the feeling there was a whole side to his wife he had not known existed. He did not like much of anything about this situation.

She said the doctor was discreet and that was why she had gone to him. She'd wanted to keep gossip out of the tabloids, but that did not explain her reticence in telling

Claudio the truth. He was her husband, but she treated him like an adversary to be warily regarded and gotten around. She did not trust him at all.

There might not be another man in her life, but Claudio did not hold the place he should rightfully hold in it, either. And if her comments over the past few days were any indication, she did not believe she held the right place in his priorities, either. Their marriage was in trouble on a wholly different level than he had suspected, but it was in trouble nonetheless.

Things were not supposed to come to this pass. He had married Therese for the express purpose of preventing that eventuality. He had chosen her not based on emotion, but because she appealed to every need he had identified in having a wife meet.

She was not meeting those needs now and had some harebrained idea of ceasing doing so altogether. She wanted to end their marriage because her body would not cooperate in her role of providing him an heir. She seemed to think he would understand and approve this so-called solution. But there was no honor in abandoning a wife because she could not have children. And he was a man who had been raised to have honor.

She would learn that a Scorsolini did not give up at the first sign of adversity.

CHAPTER NINE

THERESE was dressing when Claudio walked into their bedroom. She flicked him a quick glance and then looked away again. There was an air about him she did not want to contend with at the moment. Creases around his eyes spoke of tiredness, but the look in them spoke even more eloquently of determination.

He had made some kind of decision. And why was she so sure she was going to argue with him about it? She didn't know, but her instincts were warning her with clamoring bells to be on her guard.

His hand settled on her shoulder and she had to fight a rear-guard action against her body's natural response to his touch. She wanted to lean into him, to draw on his strength, but she'd learned the only strength she could rely on was her own.

His thumb brushed up the curve of her neck. "How are you feeling, *cara?*"

Stepping away from the insidious touch, she grimaced at the question she had heard numerous times already that day. "Fine."

He sighed and then moved to the other side of the room. "Why do I not believe you?" he asked as he started stripping out of his business suit.

"You have a suspicious mind?" she mocked without looking at him. Visual contact with his spectacular form was bad for her self-control. Even when the prospect of making love was absolutely off-limits.

"Perhaps my suspicious mind is justified," he said with an undertone she did not like.

Her gaze swung to him, but he was facing away, pulling off his shirt. Her heart accelerated as his tawny, muscular body came into view. A fierce wave of possessiveness poured through her and it was all she could do not to cross the room, touch that bare skin and declare it hers.

The primitive part of her did not recognize the practical need to end their marriage.

"What do you mean?" she asked, her voice a little high as she slid her feet into a pair of Vera Wangs.

They perfectly complemented the green sheath dress she'd chosen to wear for dinner, but their pointy toes weren't quite as comfortable. The dress was formfitting but did not rub against her abdomen and the hem stopped right above her ankles, making modest sitting easier without having to stay perfectly erect with her knees right together.

The less stress on *all* of her muscles the better.

Claudio turned around to face her, catching her ogling his body, but he didn't seem to notice.

He buttoned his shirt with deft fingers while his eyes challenged her. "You have kept a lot hidden from me in the past months. Pain you should have told me about. Excessive bleeding that could have been dangerous. I can be forgiven for not taking your word for how fine you feel at the moment."

His complacent judgment made her angry. She had been protecting him, darn it. "You want the truth?" she asked shortly and glared at him. "I'm cramping so badly I just want to lie down and die, but I'm not going to and telling you about the pain won't make it go away."

He paled at her words, but made no signs of backing down. "I cannot fix what I do not know about."

Typically arrogant Scorsolini male, thinking he had control of everything in his known universe.

She turned away from him to put on her jewelry. "You can't fix this at all."

He said nothing and she worked at putting her earrings on with trembling fingers. When she finished, she surveyed her image in the mirror critically. Her hair was down because she simply hadn't wanted to deal with putting it up, but she didn't look messy...or like she was in pain.

And for that she was grateful. She turned to leave and almost ran into him.

He steadied her with his hands on her shoulders, his expression grim. "Perhaps I cannot rid you of this condition, but I can arrange for you to lie down and have a tray brought up for your dinner."

It was so tempting, but she couldn't start giving into the endometriosis now. She'd fought too hard not to. "No."

He frowned, his eyes narrowing in disapproval. "Why not?"

"I don't want your family speculating about my health. They are under enough stress as it is."

"So are you."

"It is my choice, Claudio."

"And if I take that choice from you?"

It wasn't an idle comment. She could see it in his eyes. He would follow through with the least provocation.

"Don't threaten me."

He made a sound of disgust. "I am not threatening you. I am trying to take care of you as I should have been doing for these past several months."

Oh, no…a Scorsolini male in guilt mode was a terrifying thing. "That has never been your job, Claudio. I don't need you to take care of me. I'm not a child."

"How can you say it is not my job? You are my wife. My responsibility."

"A prince cannot look at life that way."

"This prince does."

He could have no idea how much she'd wanted to hear that sentiment months ago, but she'd already learned by then that a princess could not rely on coddling or tender loving care when she was sick. At least not from her husband. And not from anyone if she had duties to perform in the face of it.

"That's something new."

"Perhaps," he acknowledged without apology, "but it is still the right thing."

"No, it is not. It is you being stressed by everything else and adding me to your list of burdens, but I won't be added. Do you hear me? You've got enough to worry about right now without worrying about me."

"I will not dismiss you because I have other things that require my attention as well."

"Why not? You've done it before."

His mouth settled in a grim line. "That is not true."

She stepped out from under his hands. "You're welcome to your perception."

"There have been times I have had to put you second, yes, but that was because I was forced to do so by circumstance. I have never forgotten about you, or dismissed you from my thoughts or consideration."

He sounded like her believing him really mattered, but she wasn't up to an all out discussion on their marriage right now. She hadn't been exaggerating when she told him she was in pain and arguing with him wasn't making her feel loads better.

"We need to hurry, or we'll be late for dinner."

"I prefer that you stay up here and rest."

"I don't."

He sighed again. "You do not wish my family to worry about you, but it is all right for me to worry because you will not take better care of yourself?"

"I'm not doing anything that is putting my health further at risk," she said with exasperation.

"You are in pain, you should not be pushing yourself like this."

"Eating dinner with your family is hardly what I term pushing myself."

"Because you are so used to putting duty first."

"That isn't what you said in New York."

"It is exactly what I said, if you would remember. That is why your behavior shocked and worried me so much."

"You did not act worried. You acted angry." Furious, in fact.

"I *was* angry. I believed you had other reasons than your health for doing as you did."

She stopped with her hand on the doorknob, her attention arrested. What motivations could he have attributed to her behavior that would have made him as full of rage as he had been in New York? "What other reasons?"

"Nothing I wish to discuss now."

Somehow, she just knew he was hiding something… maybe even something important. "But I wish to discuss it." Then the dinner gong sounded over the intercom and she frowned. "We'll return to this after dinner."

"There is no need. It does not matter."

"It does to me." But maybe she would take her pain-killers first.

He put his arm out to her, "Shall we go?"

She took his arm, unable to stifle the zing of electricity that arced between them at the touch. "No more arguing that I am better off in bed?"

"I am conserving my energy." He opened the door and led her out into the hall.

"For what?"

"Our discussion after dinner."

"But you said you didn't want to discuss what you believed." She couldn't believe he was giving in so easily about her going to dinner or about having the conversation he was so set against.

It was so unlike him. She'd fully intended to persuade him to come clean, but she'd thought it would take a lot more effort.

"I do not, but we have other things on the agenda."

"Like what?"

"Like the fact that there will be no divorce."

There was no chance to respond as they met up with Tomasso and Maggie in the corridor and walked down together. Marcello and Danette were waiting in the drawing room when they arrived.

He smiled when he saw that Claudio was with Therese. "I am glad to see you have decided to eat a decent meal for a change."

"I have been eating," Claudio said with a frown.

"In high stress, business environments or at your desk. Time with your family is more relaxing."

Claudio smiled, making Therese's heart twist in her chest. "Are you so sure about that?"

His affection for his brothers was so strong. All she had ever wanted was for a little of that to rub off on her, but it never had and now he had some harebrained idea they had to stay married. But she knew it would be for all the wrong reasons…reasons she could not give in to.

The Scorsolini guilt gene at work, but that was not enough to carry a marriage facing the challenges theirs would. Not for long anyway.

"But of course," Marcello said drolly. "Would you deny it?"

"No," Claudio said quite seriously. "It has been a hectic week all told."

Marcello and Tomasso both nodded, frowning. Tomasso said, "I wish there was more I could do to carry Papa's burden."

"But there is not." Claudio smiled, but it was rough around the edges and Therese wondered if his brothers saw that. "I am his heir. I alone must fill many of the gaps left by his absence while in hospital."

"You are doing an amazing job," Maggie said softly, her sweet smile warming Therese despite the dragging pains in her lower pelvis.

"I forget what kind of pressure you all live under when Marcello and I are in Italy. The world seems so normal there. I can almost forget I'm married to a prince…being a tycoon is enough, I guess. But the minute we arrive here, the burden you all carry becomes apparent." Danette shook her head. "I pray it will be easier for our children." She rubbed her tummy as if comforting the baby within.

When Marcello reached over to do the same thing, something painful twisted inside Therese.

"I think it will be," Tomasso said.

"Yes," Marcello added. "You must remember, *amante*, that our baby has only a prince, not a king for a father."

"This is true," Tomasso said, "but even the children Claudio will have one day will have the benefit of more extended family to help carry the burden of office. Our father had no brothers to help carry his burden. I see a marked difference already in Gianni and Anna's childhood to our own."

"But Claudio's children will still have a harder time of it than ours will."

Tomasso agreed with a sigh. "I feel selfish in my gratitude, but I am glad that my son will not grow up to one day rule Isole dei Re."

"It's strange to think that our children will get to choose their own paths, while their cousins will have most of their future determined by their birth," Maggie said with a thoughtful frown.

"Did it bother you to know growing up that you had no choice but to be king?" Danette asked Claudio as the men led their wives into dinner.

Claudio waited until after he had seated Therese to answer. Then he looked at Danette. "I never rebelled against my future. I remember only knowing from the earliest age that one day I would be king and that that role carried with it grave responsibilities. It has meant at times that I had to put my life as an individual man aside."

Therese felt there was a message for her in his words.

"I don't envy Therese her position," Maggie said with a smile for Therese. "It's got to be hard to share your husband in such a big way with the people of his country."

Therese could not deny the words, but something was not right about them either. If Claudio loved her, she did not think sharing him with the people and problems of Isole dei Re would bother her at all.

"It is a difficult role, but my wife has always been more than equal to the task," Claudio said, approval for her lacing his voice.

She turned to face him and for several seconds the other occupants of the room seemed to fade away. There was just her and Claudio and some message was being spoken between them without words.

For no reason she could discern, tears burned the back of her eyes. "I cannot regret marrying you."

"It is not my intention that you ever shall." Then he leaned forward and did something he had never done before.

He kissed her softly and full on the lips right there in front of his family. Afterward, he straightened and began talking to his brothers as if nothing out of the ordinary had happened.

But Therese felt like her world had rocked on its axis.

Dinner was a convivial meal, but as time wore on, it became more and more difficult for her to mask her pain. She stopped eating more than a bite or two from each course after the soup. The cramping was getting very bad again, almost debilitating. Probably because she had taken nonprescription pain meds all day, not wanting to be so loopy she could not fulfill her obligations.

Perhaps she should have taken some before dinner, but she hated zoning off in the middle of conversations. And her sisters-in-law were very astute women. They would have noticed something was wrong…unlike Claudio.

Trying to find a more comfortable position, she shifted in her chair for the third time in ten minutes. Rather than make the pain more tolerable, the shift made it more acute and she had to stifle a gasp. She couldn't quite mask her wince though.

Claudio stood suddenly. "I believe Therese and I will retire early."

Tomasso frowned. "But dessert has not been served."

"We are both tired and need our rest."

He reached for Therese's arm, the expression in his eyes one of a hawk ready to swoop down on its prey. "Come. It is time you were in bed."

She knew she had no chance and therefore did not argue.

"That is not a bad idea," Tomasso said, but the look he was giving Maggie indicated sleep was the furthest thing from his mind. She blushed, but smiled back with obvious delight at his words.

Claudio waited until they were out of the room before swooping. He reached down and lifted her high against his chest with a gentle hold that made her feel secure and coddled as she had told him she did not need to be.

Liar. For it was exactly what she wanted.

"Put me down," she protested nonetheless. "I can walk." But it was so nice not to have to. "What if one of your brothers comes out and sees you carrying me like this, or one of the servants? There will be speculation."

"I never realized you were so afraid of gossip."

"I'm not."

"Then explain why all of your doctor appointments have been secret and in the States."

"I was avoiding a media frenzy."

"Gossip."

"Are you saying you aren't worried about it? You wouldn't care if the papers got word of my infertility tomorrow? I remember how upset you were with me for going to the hotel's hot tub rather than staying in my room when I took Maggie shopping in Nassau."

"You were inviting gossip then over something quite innocent. It is different to feel the need to hide a very real health problem for the sake of appearances."

"I wasn't hiding it for the sake of appearances."

"Were you not?"

"No. I just…I didn't want it to come out before we divorced. It would have made you look badly in the eyes of the public. The average person just doesn't understand what it means to be royalty."

"Since there will be no divorce, your concern was not justified."

"You're being foolishly stubborn and I don't care what you say. I don't want your family getting all worried over nothing."

"Your condition is far from nothing, but as for your current agitation. Calm yourself. Any servant who saw me carrying you like this, or my brothers for that matter, would assume I was in a hurry to have my wicked way with you."

"That's not on." Not that she didn't want him…she always did, but pain was a strong deterrent from making love.

He stopped halfway up the marble staircase and glared down at her. "Do you really believe I would try to seduce you in your current condition?"

He looked thoroughly put out with her.

She grimaced. "No, of course not. I don't know why I said it."

She really didn't. She knew in the very depths of her being that he would never willingly hurt her physically. She remembered the pains he'd taken with her virginity and felt a familiar lump of emotion form. He was such a good man and the last thing she wanted to do was let him go.

She'd spent months shoring up her defenses against him, enumerating his faults in her mind so that she would not be tempted to fight for her marriage, but all those defenses were crumbling. It was going to hurt so much to walk away from this man that she loved.

"Good, because only a selfish bastard would ignore both your period discomfort and pain to try something like that."

"I never said you were those things."

"Perhaps not in so many words…" he allowed, but the implication was clear that she had convinced him she thought that.

She stared in shock at his granitelike features as he resumed his climb up the stairs. "I have never implied I believe that about you."

"What do you call assuming divorce was the only option when you discovered you had endometriosis?"

"Practical. I call it practical." The only solution that made sense. Particularly now that she knew he had grown bored of her. Had come face-to-face with the reality that her only value to him was a sexual one. Only, even knowing that to be true, part of her heart rebelled at it.

Part of her…the very foolish part…simply refused to believe.

He said nothing, but his expression was not pretty.

Once they reached their apartments, he carried her straight through to the bedroom. "I will get your pain pills."

He laid her on the bed and then turned to get her meds. He shook two out into his hand and gave them to her. Then, like the night before, he helped her swallow them, sitting beside her and putting one arm around her shoulders for support.

She took the pills.

"Is this your version of coddling?"

"Do you feel coddled?"

Regardless of her pain, she smiled. "Yes."

"Then, yes."

"Thank you."

"Do not thank me. This should be your right."

"So, you're being so careful with me out of duty?"

"Tell me something, *cara*."

"Yes?"

"Until recent months, your response to me in bed and generosity with your body were all that a man could wish for."

"So you've said." He had valued her for them.

"Were they the result of doing your duty?"

"No, of course not. How could you ask me that?"

"As easily as you now ask if what I do for you is from duty alone."

"You don't love me, Claudio."

"I care for you. I have always cared."

"I thought so, too…in the beginning."

"What changed?"

"I don't know. Maybe nothing."

"But still you became convinced I do not care."

"You said you were bored with me."

"I was angry. It was a lie."

She didn't believe him, but bent over in an acute attack of pain before she could say so.

He lowered her to the bed. "Therese?"

The tightening in her lower abdomen relaxed some and she straightened, breathing shallowly to manage the pain.

"Is it very bad?" he asked.

"Yes."

"The hospital?"

"No."

"You are not reasonable."

"Arguing does not help me control the pain."

His jaw clenched. "We should not have gone down to dinner."

"Is that the royal we? If I recall, you were proposing I stay here to eat off a tray, not you."

"But naturally, I would have stayed with you."

There was nothing natural about it. In fact, this whole coddling thing was unnatural in their relationship. "Why?"

"You are ill."

"And you have obligations to your family."

"Which I was content to dismiss in favor of obligations related to my office for the past week. I was here at the palace for you."

"I don't understand why."

"You are my wife." He said it as if that should explain everything, but it didn't. Not by a long shot.

"I was your wife two years ago when I had the flu as well, but you didn't stay with me then. In fact, you had me moved to another room for convalescence so there was no risk of passing the bug on to you. I was your wife last year when I had a cold and you left me to the tender care of servants while you flew to Italy on business."

He looked at her like he did not understand the correlation she was trying to draw. "Those circumstances were different."

"In what way?"

"You were not in excruciating pain and we knew each ailment would run its course."

"And *duty* precluded you offering anything resembling tender loving care."

"Did you want me to become your nursemaid? I did not see that desire in you at the time. You are a very independent person when you are ill. But then I think that for all your quiet gentleness, you are an extremely independent, not to mention stubborn woman all of the time."

"Thank you for not mentioning it," she said sarcastically. "And I'm not independent."

"Oh, but you are. So independent that you have taken it upon yourself to make decisions about our marriage without consulting the other primary partner first."

"That's why I went to New York…to consult."

"A demand for a divorce is not a consultation."

"I wasn't going to start it that way, but you put me on the defensive the way you jumped down my throat for coming at all."

"I leaped to a false conclusion and was cruel to you because of it. I am sorry." He said it stiffly, like he was embarrassed, and she remembered his comment before dinner.

"What false conclusion?"

"I would prefer not to get into that."

"Too bad…just wondering what could make you look so uncomfortable is taking my mind off my cramps."

He said something she didn't get, but there was no mistaking the irritation in his manner as he scooted to sit back on the bed with his back against the headboard.

At her questioning look, he shrugged. "If you're going to grill me, I want to be comfortable."

She hid an unexpected smile. He sounded so surly.

"Tell me about your false conclusion."

CHAPTER TEN

"It was a conclusion that made sense at the time."

"You're stalling. Tell me about it."

"I believed you had found someone else."

"What?"

A dark burn washed across his sculpted cheekbones. "I became obsessed with the idea you had fallen for another man. Your demand for a divorce clinched it."

"Why?" she asked in stunned amazement.

"I could conceive of no other reason you would ask for a divorce."

"But—"

"You had started rejecting me sexually. I did not understand it."

"It hurt."

"But you did not tell me that. I had to draw my own conclusions."

"And that was that I'd taken a lover."

"I did not go that far—I could not imagine it."

"Thank you…I think."

"You had started zoning out during conversations…like you were thinking about someone else."

"My medication."

"Yes."

"I thought you didn't even notice."

"I did. Believe me."

"But you decided the reason was because my heart had become unfaithful to you, if not my body."

"I could not be sure I ever had your heart."

"What do you mean?"

"You have never said you loved me."

"Love was not a requirement of our marriage bargain."

"No, it was not."

Inexplicably she got the impression that he had wanted it to be…for her anyway. But why would he want her love when he did not feel deeply for her? It made no sense. Any more than his newfound desire to coddle her because she was sick.

Or *did* that make sense?

"I think I understand."

"I am glad."

"Not why you believed I'd found someone else." She disabused him of that notion immediately. "But I think I understand you feeling the need to coddle me now."

"Because you are ill?"

"Because you are feeling guilty for thinking I was unfaithful."

"That is not the reason I want to take care of you now."

"But you do feel guilty."

For once it was very easy to read his thoughts. They were written all over his pained features. "Yes. I should have realized you were ill."

"At least you noticed my behavior was out of the ordinary."

"Of course I noticed."

"There really ıs no *of course* about it. I thought you

didn't particularly care one way or the other that I had started saying no in the bedroom."

He looked at her like she'd lost what was left of her mind. "That is absurd. Naturally I cared, but I was not going to be a petulant child about it. A woman's no is no."

"And why I said no wasn't important?"

"Of course it was important."

"But you would rather think me guilty of immorality than to ask."

"I did ask."

Then she remembered. "And I didn't want to talk about it, but it had been going on for months. Why wait so long?"

He shifted on the bed, his face a study in hard angles and stonelike passivity. "It stung my pride for you to reject me sexually. To talk about it would have made it worse. I would have felt like I was begging for your favors."

"That's absurd."

"It is not absurd. It is truth. Why do you think I was gone so many months during your period?"

"Because it was convenient."

"You do not think much of me, do you?"

"That's not true."

"I believe it is, but it is not the issue under debate, so we will leave it. I organized my travel plans to coincide with your monthly because you made it clear that even light touching during your monthly made you feel uncomfortable. I find it a real challenge to keep my hands off you and the best solution was to be gone from our bed completely. You can believe me, or not…but I organized my schedule for your sake, not my own."

"You have no problem not touching me outside the bedroom."

"If you truly think that, you are blind. I would touch you all the time, but it is not seemly for a king to be that way with his wife."

"You aren't a king yet."

"But I will be. And because of my position, I have set standards for my own behavior. Achieving those standards challenges me, especially where you are concerned. The only place I gave myself permission to be completely free with you was our bedroom. I found it very difficult to police my behavior in there as well," he said as if admitting a grave sin.

"I didn't realize…."

"In my own defense, I thought you knew."

"How could I?"

"I thought my desire for you was obvious."

"It wasn't obvious when you took no so easily and acted as if nothing was different between us. I thought it didn't matter."

"Now you know differently."

"I know that sex is a key element in our relationship, yes."

"You say that like it is a bad thing."

She bit her lip and looked away. How honest should she be? Her marriage was over even if he wasn't willing to recognize that. Was there any use in rehashing old hurts? Then again, hadn't she spent enough of her marriage hiding from him?

She turned her head so their gazes met. "I wanted you to care for me on a level that was more personal than the sexual."

"What is more intimate than sex?"

"I'm not sure how to explain it," she admitted. "It's just that I wanted to be important to you for my own sake…not only because of the pleasure you found in my body, or even how well I did my job as your wife."

"You want me to love you."

"Maybe." She shrugged. "Maybe nothing less than love would have satisfied me, but it doesn't matter anymore."

"You no longer want my love? Is that why you fight my coddling as you call it? You are content to do without me?"

"I don't mean to fight your attention," she said around a yawn as the pain meds started taking serious effect. "It's just come as such a surprise."

The truth was she liked it. Too much. If she let herself get used to it, it was going to be that much harder to walk away, but she couldn't seem to summon the necessary will-power to keep rejecting it, either.

"I'm glad you're here with me right now," she said softly. "Even if you should probably be somewhere else. I know you have too many other responsibilities right now to be worrying about me, but I can't help enjoying the attention. I suppose that makes me weak."

She was speaking to herself really, but he answered.

"No, it does not. It makes you human." He seemed pleased about something, but she couldn't imagine what.

She sighed. "I guess, but you can't afford to take the time to be calling me several times a day, or to keep playing nursemaid."

"You must stop trying to take care of everyone else in the world. I can well afford the time for phone calls and if I do not care for you, who will? You refuse to tell anyone of your condition."

He had a point, but she couldn't leave it there. He was trying to make everything sound so easy and it wasn't. Only her muddled brain was having a hard time remembering why exactly. She remembered one thing.

"You didn't have time for phone calls before."

"I did…until you stopped answering all my calls."

She stared at him, remembering through the mist trying to cloud her mind. What he said was true. He used to call her several times a day, no matter where he was in the world. There had rarely been any more discernible reason for the phone call than to connect briefly. He would ask about something on her schedule or give her a short run-down on his latest meeting. In fact, a lot of communication she took for granted had happened during those calls. It was only when he stopped making them that she realized it. She had started ignoring some of his calls and even cutting him off when she did answer…because he wasn't saying the right thing. "It felt like you were only checking on my role as your princess. The calls were too impersonal."

And that hurt, but then so had having him stop making them.

"How could I have made them more personal?"

Looking back, she saw that for him those calls had been personal, his way of being with her when duty kept them apart so frequently. Her throat tightened with emotion.

"You could have told me…just once…that you missed me."

"I am sorry I did not spell it out. I thought the calls them-selves would give you that message."

"You called me because you missed me?" she asked, even now shocked by the concept.

"*Sì.* For what other reason would I have called and dis-cussed such inconsequential matters?"

"I don't know. My brain is getting fuzzy."

He frowned and got up from the bed.

"If you follow the pattern from last night, you will not be cognizant enough to converse at all in about twenty minutes and there is something I wish to discuss before that happens."

"It was worse last night because I'd lost so much blood and gotten so little sleep," she said woozily.

"If you say so." He began pulling her shoes off. "You have said that surgery is the prescribed cure for endometriosis?"

"Not a cure exactly, but close. It's my best chance for living a fairly normal, pain-free life." She watched as he put her shoes aside and then rolled down her thigh-highs. His eyes flared with hunger as he looked at her exposed legs, but his touch was almost completely impersonal.

"What do they do? They only have to remove your reproductive system?"

At least this conversation was easy. She'd researched the alternatives so thoroughly, she thought she could recite them and their benefits or detriments in her sleep.

"No. Not anymore. They can actually usually remove the growths of tissue through laser surgery. Recovery time is minimal and I don't even have to stay overnight in the hospital afterward."

"But you will."

"I *will?*" she asked delicately, her eyes narrowing.

The look he gave her from his brown eyes said she could argue all she liked, but his mind was made up. "Even laser surgery carries risk and is traumatic to the body. I do not agree with this move in the medical community of dismissing a patient from care too early."

"I'm sure insurance companies have more to do with that than doctor preferences. If you are willing to pay for it, I have no doubt the hospital will happily keep me in residence." She wondered if doing so would help assuage his guilt.

"And this surgery…it is a guaranteed fix?"

"No, but like I said…it's my best chance. A high percentage of the women who elect to have the surgery end up having it again sometime down the road."

"It seems a small price to pay if it will alleviate the kind of pain and bleeding you have been having."

"That's how I see it."

He was taking her dress off and she was letting him. No matter what she said to the contrary it felt wonderful having him care for her like this. Especially knowing that soon he would not be there to even scrub her back in a sexy shower.

He did not offer to get her a gown, but said, "Do you need to fix things up for the night?"

She swung her legs over the side of the bed. "Yes."

But before she could stand up on her own, he was once again lifting her and carrying her into the en suite. He left her to take care of things and was undressed and in bed, his laptop and papers scattered around him when she returned to the bedroom.

"You don't have to go to bed just because I am."

"It is no hardship after the week I had, I assure you."

She nodded, too sluggish from the pain meds to argue further. "Will you at least try to go to sleep before midnight?"

"Do you want me to?" he asked as if the idea pleased him.

"Yes. I don't want you having a heart attack like your dad."

"That would be unfortunate, would it not? After all, who would run our country if we were both convalescing?"

"The mind boggles, but I wasn't thinking about the good of Isole dei Re," she said more candidly than she would have if she wasn't slightly loopy from the pills. "I worry about you. I l—um…I'm going to sleep."

She climbed into the bed, unable to believe she had almost blurted out her love for him.

* * *

Claudio worked beside the sleeping Therese, his mind split between his duties and his wife. If she but knew it, that was not such an uncommon state of affairs. But to hear her tell it, she mattered to him only in a very peripheral way.

And he had allowed her to believe so. It had been a conscious decision, but he had not foreseen the consequences. He had been protecting himself from taking his father's path. He'd never wanted a love that could turn a strong man into a cheat. After the talk with his father in the hospital, perhaps he understood what had driven Vincente so many years ago, but with understanding did not come peace.

The result was the same. Love made fools of men.

But had denying the tender emotion in his relationship with Therese been any big improvement over the vulnerability love caused? He still felt vulnerable…he still felt fear at the prospect of losing her. That was no improvement…and after his erroneous conclusion drawn from her behavior, he felt a fool.

Worse than a fool, he felt like a cruel monster. It had never been his intention that Therese should be hurt by marriage to him. He had believed he was offering her a good life and had thought he would make a good husband. Not a normal husband—a king in the making could not be that—but a good one regardless.

He had not anticipated the current events, but even so…to have failed so miserably at his first real test in the husband department was galling. He did not take failure well. He never had, which was why he worked so hard to avoid it. But there was no denying that he had misjudged his wife and in misjudging her, he had added to her suffering.

He had also destroyed fragile bonds that if he did not repair were going to result in the end of his marriage. He would not accept that, but he was not sure what to do to fix the problem. He felt helpless and that was not a pleasant feeling.

A prince in line to the throne should not be helpless.

He would not be if she cared for him…her love would be a tie that could bind them together, even if he'd made a few rather ugly errors of judgment. But she did not love him. Though, for a second there…just before she had gone to sleep, he had thought she was going to say she loved him. And he had wanted to hear the words. Very much.

She had not said them, though, and he could not help wondering if it had all been a figment of his imagination. Even if she had loved him once, and he thought that was possible, she loved him no longer.

Why did that knowledge hurt so much?

As she had pointed out. Love was not part of their marriage bargain.

But he wanted her love. He…needed it. Somehow, he would convince her to stay married…and perhaps in doing so, give himself another chance at the love that had warmed his very soul before he realized it was ever there. She had married him loving him and only now, looking back, could he recognize that.

She probably thought he did not care, but she was wrong. He cared very much. She was wrong, too, about divorce being the only solution to their dilemma. Just as she had been wrong that his phone calls hadn't meant he missed her. Only now did he recognize how many things she had taken the wrong way and he did not know how to fix that, either.

He had been trained to be a ruler among men, he had not been taught how to soothe a woman's emotions, how to convince her of his affection. He and Therese did not see the world in the same way and he had made the mistake of believing they did. Because of the way she had been raised. But she was still a woman, different from him and her thinking steeped in a logic that was no kind of logic to him.

He'd taken for granted that she knew many things that in retrospect he had to admit had not been as obvious to her as they were to him. He could not be sure if that was a man-woman thing, or something unique to their personalities, but it did not matter either way. She had made faulty assumptions just as he had. If he could admit the fault of his own reasoning, and everyone accepted he had a corner share of the market on stubborn, she could, too.

"You've got to be kidding. Having the procedure right now is impossible."

In a rare moment of solitude, Therese had been relaxing in one of her favorite spots on the manicured grounds behind the palace when Claudio had tracked her down. The sun warmed her while a gentle breeze ruffled her long hair. It was lovely and peaceful…or it had been. Now she had six feet four inches of masculine energy vibrating down at her.

Claudio sat down on the bench beside her, his vitality calling to her senses on a level that had nothing to do with logic or reasoning. "The doctor said there was no problem with you having the surgery as soon as your monthly is over and that should be within the next couple of days."

She was not used to these frank discussions they had been having when for almost three years, the only earthy talk that ever happened between them was in bed. Even then, there were things she simply would not discuss. He'd blown the lid off the taboos in their marriage when he'd taken care of her the other night and seemed to have no desire to go back to the more circumspect relationship they had once shared.

Accepting that truth with what grace she could muster, she argued, "That's not the only thing to consider. Your father is coming home from the hospital today and he will be convalescing for a while yet."

Claudio tensed, his mouth sliding into a frown. "Are you saying you prefer to wait until his health is completely restored?" he asked with disbelief.

"Well, at least until he is well enough to begin taking over some of his duties again."

"That will be six weeks from now," he said grimly.

"Yes, I know."

Claudio cupped her nape, his face set in stern lines. "I will not allow you to go through another period like this last one."

"It is my body." But the words came out breathy. His touch was doing things to her and he wasn't even meaning to, she was sure of it.

Though casual affection was another thing she was not used to from him and didn't know what to make of it now.

"*Sì.* It is your body…a beautiful, generous body that it is my privilege and responsibility to ensure you care for adequately."

"You're my husband, not my father."

"Your father would have ignored your pain. I will not."

He was right, but somehow that memory did not have the power to hurt her as it once had. "I don't want *your* father upset."

Claudio moved his touch from her nape to take her hand in his. He aligned their fingers, his long tanned ones dwarfing hers. "Your hands are so small, so delicate…so beautiful."

The breath froze in her chest for a second and then she inhaled as her heart started tripping. He had commented many times when they were making love how much he adored having her hands on him, but never had he said anything outside the bedroom. "Um…your dad…"

Claudio clasped her hand in his and smiled, disconcerting her further. "Vincente is fine. At my request, he has spent several days longer in the hospital than the doctor initially recommended. During that time, he has been on bed rest and restricted from the phone, but he has been up and about, walking the corridors and visiting other patients since two days after the surgery. He is well on his way to recovery."

"But he's still weak."

"Do not let him hear you say that."

Therese had to acknowledge the justness of that warning. "It's all Flavia can do to keep him in the hospital and resting for long periods."

"Precisely. He would not thank you for trying to protect him at your own expense. I only thank God Mamacita decided now was the time to come back into his life because I do not think the rest of us would have been so successful."

"They're a good couple."

"Yes. It is too bad they took so long to figure that truth out."

"Infidelity isn't something you can easily dismiss."

"Not my father in himself or Flavia in him, I know…but she seems to have come to terms with the past as has he."

"I'm glad." She loved both proud people and was so happy they had found each other again.

"I also, but do not think you are going to derail this conversation. I have spoken to your doctor in Miami and he has agreed to fly here in four days to perform the operation."

"You had no right to call him," she gritted. "And I do not want to have the procedure here."

Claudio glared right back at her, all affability gone, but his hold on her hand was still gentle…as if even in his anger he was cherishing her. "*You* had no right to keep your condition a secret from me. You could have had the surgery months past but for your attempts to do so."

"I told you why I did that."

"I do not agree with your reasons. You should have told me. This is the truth."

She looked out over the grounds. They were sheltered from a view of the palace by trees and shrubbery, but she could see the spires rising above the treetops. "You are too arrogant for words sometimes."

"Only sometimes?"

She laughed. She couldn't help it. He was so unapologetic, but he was being bossy for her benefit. Not to hurt her and deep in her heart she knew that. "It only makes me mad enough to spit nails *sometimes.*"

"I cannot imagine you spitting anything, my proper little wife." He spoke close to her ear, his lips settling in a gentle kiss against her temple before he pulled his head back.

It was a full three seconds before she could respond. Because she knew she had to fight the impact of that kiss, she forced herself to dwell on the unpleasant side of reality. "A proper wife could give you a child. I won't be able to and if I have the surgery here, the whole world will know about it. You'll be labeled heartless and selfish when we divorce."

In a totally unexpected move, he grabbed her by the waist and lifted her onto his lap, then cupped her face so she had no choice but to meet his eyes. "There will be no divorce and if you attempt to leave me, I will be labeled worse than that."

"What do you mean?" she asked and was embarrassed by how weak her voice sounded.

"You will not leave me, Therese."

"You're not talking kidnapping…you can't be." But by the look in his eyes, she could tell he *was* thinking about it. "That's ridiculous, Claudio. You are not one of your marauding ancestors."

"Who says my ancestors were marauders?"

"They were pirates, plain and simple. They used their ill-gotten bounty to establish a country, but they were not the pillars of society their descendants became."

"Are you saying I am a pirate beneath my layers of civility?" he asked, sounding an awful lot exactly like that.

"No…I am attempting to remind you that you are one of those rational, civilized descendants." She looked into his eyes and what she read there made her shiver.

"I would have agreed with you…before, but in the last weeks, I have discovered a heretofore unknown streak of primitive possessiveness where you are concerned that hearkens back to my ancestors quite effectively."

"So you do realize it's there…"

"Yes. And you must also, which then means you should realize how foolish it would be to attempt to leave me."

She glared at his complacent certainty. "If I decide to walk, I will walk."

She meant it, too. Maybe she didn't descend from Sicilian pirates, but she had the blood of Romans running in her veins as well as a good dose of American assertiveness.

CHAPTER ELEVEN

"DO NOT decide to walk." The pleading in his voice was more astonishing than the fact he'd allowed his primitive streak to show so blatantly.

"What will you do?" she asked softly, trying to read his expression, but not understanding what she saw there.

He was silent several seconds and then he sighed. "Follow you."

She laughed because it was absurd. He was more proud than his father and if Vincente had been unable to bend enough to apologize for behavior he had known was reprehensible, Claudio would never stoop to chasing after a wayward wife. Besides, he couldn't, even if he wanted to. "Your duties wouldn't allow it and you would never lower yourself to tagging after me like a lost puppy."

"Puppies are harmless. I am not. Make no mistake…I would follow you."

"But your duty—"

"My first duty is to you, my wife…and to our marriage. I will not let you go."

He would…if she really wanted to go. Primitive streak, or not…he was a modern man. But what he was saying here was that he would not make it easy. She didn't know if she

had the strength to fight both him and her own desire to stay.
However, she wasn't sure anymore, either, if she had the
strength to stay in a marriage in which she was not loved.

It hurt, as much or more than the endometriosis. She'd
learned something last night. Her pain and vulnerability
that resulted from loving where the feeling was not returned had made her misinterpret his actions, thereby adding more hurt to her beleaguered heart. Without his love,
wouldn't she continue to do that very thing?

No matter how much she might want to avoid it.

She laid her hand over the one against her cheek. "You
have to be reasonable about this. Please, Claudio."

"I am not the one being unreasonable here. It is both
foolish and dangerous for you to wait to have the surgery.
And it is criminally shortsighted for you to believe we
must divorce."

"I am infertile. I cannot give you an heir."

"Your doctor said that IVF had a seventy percent success rate with endometriosis patients."

"That is still not a guarantee."

"Neither is unhindered fertility."

"But there's a better chance for you to have children
with a woman who does not have endometriosis."

"I do not want another woman!"

She dropped her hand and leaned back with a jerk,
stunned by his vehemence. "That's just guilt talking."

He shook his head, barely banked rage glittering in his
dark gaze. "It is not guilt. You are my wife. I want you to
remain my wife. If there is no other man, why are you so
intent on ending our marriage?"

"There is no other man," she exclaimed. "I can't believe
we are back to that."

"Then why?"

"It's for the good of the country, Claudio. You would see that if you were thinking with your brain and not your pride."

"No." He glowered. "The good of the country is best served by you staying as my wife."

She couldn't believe he was being so stubborn. "Not if I can't give you children."

"If you cannot, I have brothers and a nephew who are in line to the throne."

"You heard your brothers last night. They don't want their children to have the pressures of growing up to be king."

"Tough," he said without the slightest hint of apology. "While they may not have been born first, they *were* born to a king. If I were to die before having a child, Tomasso would have to take my role and his son would then inherit the throne. It is the way of our bloodline."

She put both her hands on his chest, needing the feel of his warmth under her fingers. "Don't talk about dying."

"Do not talk about leaving me."

"It isn't the same thing."

"No. It is worse, for a man does not choose when he may die but you are talking about willfully killing our marriage and removing yourself from my life."

"For your own good. *Don't you understand that?*" she appealed in a choked voice.

"I understand you believe it is for my good, but you are wrong."

"But—"

"Stop arguing with me. You made a lifetime commitment to me, Princess Therese Scorsolini. I will not let you break it. I will not let you leave me."

"You can't stop me."

"I can. Even if you walk away, I will not remarry. There will be no other chance at heirs for me."

"Once the divorce is final, you'll change your mind," she said, hurting because she was sure it was true.

"There will be no divorce. Perhaps I am not so archaic that I will physically keep you against your will, but there will be no other marriage for either of us."

"You can't stop it."

"I may be powerless to stop some things, my intransigent little wife, but we are talking the divorce laws of Isole dei Re here, not American law. You cannot divorce a member of the royal family without their consent. I will not give it. Ever."

"*That* is archaic."

"Perhaps." He shrugged, obviously not in the least offended by that judgment. "But it is our law. And we were married here, Therese…not in the States. Remember that."

"But—"

"There are no buts." He seemed supremely pleased by that statement, as if a great weight had been lifted from his shoulders.

She didn't understand it. Surely marriage to her was the weight. "You want to be a father."

He smiled and one hand settled gently over her lower abdomen. "Yes, and I would like nothing more than for you to carry my child, but we can adopt if you cannot conceive. You will be such a good mother once you get this notion of divorce out of your head."

"We can't adopt," she gasped. "What about progenitor?"

"Of course we can. As for the ascension to the throne, I will have to name my nephew my successor, but it can be done. We are modern royalty, not one of my ancestors."

"This from the man who just told me he was sticking with an archaic law to keep me married to him?"

"I have had enough of this talk of divorce." He carefully lifted her from his lap and set her on the bench. Then he stood up and looked down at her, his eyes filled with censure. "You are one of the most compassionate people I know, but you do not seem to care when you stomp with hobnailed boots all over my feelings and my ideals. If all you wanted was a sperm donor when you married, why did you not go to a sperm bank instead?"

"What?" Had he lost his mind? "I don't think of you as a sperm donor!"

"But the moment you discover I cannot get you pregnant you are ready to divorce me."

"Not for my sake, *for yours,*" she stressed, but she was beginning to doubt the validity of her own arguments.

He patently did not want a divorce. Whether it was guilt, a sense of responsibility, pride or just plain physical desire not spent that was prompting him, he wanted to stay married…to her. She'd never anticipated this reaction.

He was still glaring down at her. "It is not for my sake if it will make me unhappy."

"*Would* divorcing me make you unhappy?"

"What the blasted hell do you think I have been saying here?"

She stared at him, totally unsure what to say.

"Say something."

"I'm in shock."

"And that makes me angry. What have I done to make you believe our marriage meant nothing to me?"

"We married for convenience. It wasn't about love. I

knew that when you asked me to be your wife. I fit your requirements. All of them."

"You are right…I married you because you were the ideal woman for me. That being the case, what made you determine I have no feelings for you? Of course I do." But he looked like the words shocked him, as if he was having some kind of major inner revelation.

She refused to speculate about what that could be. She'd hurt herself too much already believing in moonshine and manmade miracles.

"You are everything I wanted in a woman and more, *cara*," he said more quietly.

"But you don't love me."

"What is love, if it is not what we have?"

That at least, she had a definitive answer for. "It's what your brothers have with their wives. I've seen a Scorsolini male in love…first Tomasso, then Marcello and even lately your father with Flavia. *It is not the way you are with me*."

"So, what is it you think I feel for you?"

"Desire. I think you like me…or at least you used to. I think you feel guilty now…because you wish you'd noticed my condition before, and maybe even because you were so cruel about the divorce before you knew why I had suggested it."

"But you are certain I do not love you?"

"Yes."

"I suppose that makes us even," he said on a sigh. "But things are about to change around here."

With that he turned and walked away.

With King Vincente's return to the palace, things were too hectic the rest of that day for Therese to think much about

Claudio's final statement in the garden. However, that night when she was alone in their apartments while he attended a function in his father's stead, her mind chewed on it endlessly.

She had suggested she should go with him to the State dinner, but Claudio had refused and no amount of arguing on her part would change his mind. She had even had to assure him that she was feeling much better, which she was, before he had been willing to go himself. Which was a hundred and eighty degree turn around for him.

Duty came first, last and always for Claudio Scorsolini. *Or it had*...maybe it still did. He said his duty to her as his wife was of primary importance, but it hadn't always been that way. She knew it hadn't. There was too much evidence to the contrary. What had changed? Or, maybe she was tipping at windmills to think anything really had. Only, was guilt really strong enough of a motivator to make someone as entrenched in his responses to life as Claudio change so much? It seemed a stretch, even for a Scorsolini.

Equally as important, what had he *meant* in the garden?

In saying they were even did he mean that he agreed with her and that *he* didn't think he loved her, either? Or was he saying that he didn't believe *she* loved him? And in either case...what did he mean that things were going to change? No matter how she looked at it, the implication was that love was entering into their marriage bargain...by Claudio's say so.

Despite her final plea to the contrary, he told his family about her condition the next day. He also told them that she would be having surgery for it, and how soon. In a move that was again totally out of character, he had gone on to tell them that while surgery would hopefully take care of her symptoms, enough damage had already been done to her female organs that without IVF, she was for all intents and purposes infertile.

His brothers and father were clearly stunned by his openness, but the other women treated the news as if it was something that the whole family should know. But just as Therese had thought it would, the news caused a minor uproar in the family with Flavia taking it hardest of all.

She and King Vincente were sitting together on the butternut-yellow suede leather sectional sofa in the family reception room.

The family reception room was the only one in the palace that was decorated with comfortable modern furniture. Therese had insisted on disposing of the formal pieces and furnishing the room in warm tones and comfortable seating arrangements. King Vincente had informed her that the two recliners she'd had installed were the only ones that had ever been allowed in the palace. A month after the room was finished, he requested a recliner for his own apartments as well.

She'd wanted a place to congregate comfortably as a family once their children came along. It had been important to her to raise her sons and daughters with a sense of normalcy pocketed into every aspect of their lives. She'd wanted warmth and togetherness to be a natural part of their lives, not an anathema. The Scorsolinis were warm and loving people and cooperated with her despite their royal heritage.

Everyone was in there now except Tomasso's children, who had gone to bed already. King Vincente should probably have been sleeping as well, but that was not an option.

While he had been willing to sit with his feet up on the chaise lounge at one end of the sectional, he had drawn the line at being sent to bed like a child as he had put it. Flavia had grumbled, but she had fussed around him to make sure he was comfortable and then taken her seat beside him.

Therese was sitting on the part of the sectional catty-corner to her mother-in-law. Claudio had pulled her down to sit beside him rather than allowing her to take an armchair which was her normal habit. Then he'd draped his arm over her shoulders with casual possessiveness. It felt nice, if a bit strange.

Tomasso was seated in one of the recliners with Maggie settled snugly in his lap. Which was a lot more intimate…so Therese was not embarrassed. Marcello and Danette were at the other end of the sectional, his arm around her waist and her back against his body rather than the sofa.

Flavia's beautiful dark eyes filled with stricken emotion. "I knew something was wrong, but I hesitated to say anything. I am so sorry. Many times, you must have been in pain and hiding it."

Therese couldn't deny it, but she didn't want her mother-in-law to feel guilty because of it. It was hardly Flavia's fault that the endometriosis was so painful. Or anyone else's for that matter.

She reached out to touch Flavia's hand. "It's all right. Saying something would not have made a difference."

"On the contrary, had we known sooner, your treatment could have happened sooner."

She glared sideways at Claudio. "It's hardly your mother's fault."

"I did not say it was, but had you said something earlier,

it would have been better for your own sake and much could have been avoided between us."

She couldn't believe he was saying that in front of his family. "Let's not get into that right now," she hissed.

"If that is your wish, but it is the truth."

She couldn't quite stifle her sigh of irritation.

Tomasso made a choking sound on the other side of the room and Maggie nudged him with her elbow.

"What is so amusing, *fratello mio?*"

"Therese is frowning at you."

"You find this funny?" Claudio asked, sounding far from amused himself.

"You must admit, it is not like her," Marcello said, his own eyes shimmering with amusement.

Therese looked at both brothers and wondered what had gotten into them. "You think the fact I am upset with my husband is a joke?" she asked with a puzzled frown.

They were both usually more sensitive than that. They were Scorsolini men, which meant they weren't the most intuitive when it came to emotions, but this was odd even for them.

Danette bit her lip and then smiled with a shrug. "You've got to admit, it isn't like you, hon."

"The day your father and Claudio grilled me, you were really annoyed with them, but you were so subtle about it. The classic princess." Maggie grimaced. "I was sort of awed by you, to tell the truth."

Therese didn't know what to say. They were all right… she was not hiding her emotions as well as she used to. But why should they find that *funny?*

"When you are annoyed with my brother, you do not hide that fact," Claudio said to Maggie.

"Not in front of family, no," Maggie agreed with a rueful smile.

"You can say that again," Tomasso said with a laugh and promptly received another playful elbow to his ribs.

Ignoring the byplay, Claudio turned to look down at Therese. "Our marriage is not so different from theirs."

In that moment, when he was behaving toward her very much the way his brothers were toward their wives, she wasn't sure what to say…if anything to refute that statement.

"No, I do not think your marriage is so different," Flavia said, her expression stern. "But I had wondered when *you* would wake up to that fact, my son."

"I assure you, I am very awake to it now," Claudio replied allowing his gaze to flick momentarily to his stepmother, apparently not in the least offended by her censure.

It almost seemed as if there was another level of silent communication going on between them. Like this discussion was not entirely new to them.

But Therese gasped. *Was he trying to imply he loved her?*

His focus returned to her, his eyes filled with wary vulnerability. "What? You have not noticed the similarities?"

"No…um…I hadn't."

Flavia shook her head. "That is not surprising after your upbringing, but child, you must stop looking at our Claudio through the eyes of a diplomat's daughter and begin to see him with the eyes of a woman who is willing to trust his heart and her own."

Flavia had her full attention now. "What do you mean, considering my upbringing?"

"You have not known unconditional love…I think in fact, you have known very little love at all. You are used to assuming it is not there, when in fact, it is."

For no reason she could discern, Therese's chest tightened with emotion. "I don't understand."

"We all love you, that is all I am saying." Flavia squeezed Therese's hand.

Tomasso smiled. "Yes, and while I would be honored to have my son one day sit on the Scorsolini throne, I cannot help hoping IVF works for you two."

"Because you don't want him to know the pressure of ruling a kingdom?" Therese asked, painfully uncertain of the rightness of staying married to Claudio.

"Because any child born to you and my brother will be very blessed and a beautiful addition to this world."

"That is a lovely thing to say and quite true besides." Flavia smiled her approval on Tomasso and then turned to adjust the blanket covering King Vincente's legs.

"Stop fussing, *amore*. I am fine." The king reached out and brushed a finger down Flavia's cheek. "So long as you stay with me, I am fine."

Flavia smiled, her eyes filled with obvious love, but said nothing.

"Is this where you two announce you are getting married again?" Danette asked, her hazel eyes alight with pleased speculation.

Incredibly, Flavia blushed and sent an uncertain look at each of her sons. The king just grinned. "Yes, my children that is exactly what happens next."

"That is wonderful! When is the wedding?" Marcello asked.

"In three month's time…when it is safe to have a wedding night," King Vincente replied with a roguish look at Flavia. "Though I tried to convince your mother six weeks was sufficient, she was adamant."

A real blush now staining her cheeks, she slapped his arm gently. "We have waited more than two decades to be together that way again, we can wait a few additional weeks so my worries are set at rest."

After that, hugs and kisses of congratulations ensued. The attention was firmly removed from Therese and Claudio, for which she was eternally grateful.

Later, she was lying awake in the dark, her mind spinning with what Flavia had implied and the strange way Claudio had been behaving. Even now, he slept facing her, his head above hers on the pillow, one hand on her shoulder, the other resting lightly on her hip and his calf slung over hers. She was wrapped up as if he was afraid she would get away.

"Explain to me how you believe a Scorsolini man in love behaves." His deep voice coming out of the dark startled her.

"I thought you were asleep."

"I am not."

"Apparently."

"So, tell me."

"Why?"

"Please, *tesoro mio,* do not play games with me."

"I'm not trying to, but I don't understand where this is coming from."

"You told me you were sure I did not love you because I am not the husband to you that my brothers are to the women they love. I want to know how in specific terms I have failed."

She felt like she couldn't breathe. "Why?"

"So I can fix it."

"You want me to believe you love me?" she asked softly.

"Is that not obvious?"

"Maybe it should be, but no…it's not really."

"It is as Flavia said…you are so unused to receiving love, you do not recognize it when it is around you."

"I want to be loved," she admitted with a vulnerability she would never have shown him before the watershed of events in the past two weeks.

"I do love you, Therese, and one day you will know it."

No, it wasn't possible, but why was he saying it? Guilt could prompt a lot of things, but not a false confession of love from him. She didn't think. "Are you saying you love me because you think you have to…are you trying to make up for something?"

"No." That was all. A simple no. He didn't get all offended, or cranky, or try to convince her with more words.

And there was something incredibly convincing about that simplicity.

"I…"

"You are unsure. I understand this. I did not realize I loved you when I married you. You can be forgiven for not being aware of it as well. Flavia noticed, but she also saw that I was fighting it. *Porca miseria*…I was so foolish, I did not even see your love for me, but I noticed when it was gone."

"Gone?" she asked faintly, tipping her head back so she could see his face.

Or at least the shadow of it in the darkness of the room.

She could feel his gaze burning into her even though he could not see her any better in the dark than she could see him. "Yes, gone. Did you think I would not notice? I assure you, I am not quite that unobservant. The way you used to look at me as if I was all you could ever want…the way you lit up when I came into a room. It is gone." His voice was laced with a pain she understood only too well. "I only pray that with God's help and the advice of my family, I will be able to earn it back again."

"You've asked your family…your *brothers* for advice… on winning my love?" she asked in total shock.

"Yes, though neither seems particularly smart on the subject." Claudio sounded very disgruntled by that truth.

"What did they say?"

"Tomasso suggested I woo you in bed, but that is not an option and I do not want to wait until it is to convince you."

"Oh…"

"Marcello suggested I talk honestly with you, but I have been doing that for days now and it does no good."

"Honest communication is necessary to a strong relationship." But the person you were communicating with had to believe you and not second-guess your motives… like she had been doing with his.

Could it be true? Did he love her? She'd been wrong about so many things and so had he, but he apparently wanted to fix his shortcomings. He wanted her to feel loved.

"That is what Flavia said, but Papa thinks you need proof. Again, I did not find that very useful. I do not know what proof to give you."

She actually smiled at the disgruntled tone in his voice. "Your brothers had no suggestions for that?"

"As I said, nothing I could use."

"Bed is not the only place to express love." But she saw now that it had been the place he had been most comfortable doing so.

"I know this. I reserved all my affection and the release of my emotions for the bedroom, but that only convinced you your primary use to me was as a bedmate. And it isn't, *amore*. Please believe that you have always mattered to me on every level a woman can impact a man. I could slice out my own tongue for some of the things I said after you told me you thought we needed a divorce. You believed every one of them too easily, but then you could not believe me when I told you they were prompted by temper and hurt, not truth. I had been too negligent as a husband and had convinced you too strongly of my lack of feelings for you to easily believe I have them for you now. I did not realize any of this until it was too late."

"Too late?"

"I woke up to many things too late." The sadness in his voice was too real, too deep to ignore.

He really did love her. He hadn't realized it and in typical Claudio fashion, had been intent on not being controlled by his emotions. But he realized it now and he was hurting.

Just as she had been hurting.

She felt like his agony was inside her own heart. And conversely, she thought that if she asked...he would say he could also feel the pain that had been causing more internal hemorrhaging inside her than the endometriosis. Because he loved her and her pain was his pain.

The evidence had been there all along, but she'd attributed every motive under the sun except the true one...that he loved her.

She turned on her side to face him fully and reached up to press the button above their bed that turned on dim lights. They cast a golden glow over his features, revealing glittery dark orbs and telltale wetness on his temple.

She reached out and touched it, unable to believe that he was crying for her. Men like Claudio did not cry. Not ever.

"It isn't too late," she whispered.

The big body curled so protectively around hers went rigid, his gorgeous face contorted with a hope it was painful for her to see. "It is not?"

"No."

"Wha…" He swallowed and took a deep breath and then let it out. "What exactly are you trying to say here?"

"I wondered what made Danette so special…why she could be loved by her parents, by Marcello, but I was destined not to be loved by the people that mattered most to me."

"Danette is special, but, Therese…to me you are infinitely more precious. I do love you and I will spend the rest of my life proving it. Your parents are two rather stupid people."

"They aren't. They're both very smart."

"Not when it comes to love. You are incredible and to have you in my life is my greatest blessing. That they could not recognize that very thing makes them idiots."

"You didn't recognize it as first…"

"I did, but I did not label the feelings you evoked in me love because to my mind that made me dangerously vulnerable."

"Like your father."

"*Sì.*"

"We all learn things from our parents."

"But we can unlearn them, too. I have. I love you, Therese, and that does not make me a fool or weak. It gives me strength and it fills me with pleasure when I think of one day sharing that love with you. And we will, Therese. Because even if you won't tell me what it is my brothers do, I will figure it out and I will do it and you will know you are loved."

"You want to stay married to me even if it means not having your own son inherit the throne of Isole dei Re."

"*Sì*. This is true. You finally believe me?"

"Oh, I believe you…" And the belief was making her giddy. "I love you, Claudio. Yesterday, today and forever."

The hand curled around her hip convulsed, grabbing her in an almost painful grip. "You can't."

"I can and I do." She took her own deep breath and then plunged into a pool she had never swum in before. "I believe you love me, too. I really do."

"I do love you, my precious wife. I do. Thank God you believe me…thank God." He closed his eyes as if sending those thanks on the wings of angels and then opened them again. "From this point forward you will never again have cause to doubt it. I give you my word as a prince."

"I believe you," she said again, her heart burbling with a kind of happiness she had never known.

He leaned forward and kissed her. It was the most poignant meeting of their lips they had ever known, for it affirmed in a wholly nonsexual way that they were two halves of one whole. Always.

EPILOGUE

THE surgery was a complete success and, miraculously, so was the IVF procedure performed two months later. Therese's doctor was shocked it had worked on the first try, but she wasn't. After discovering Claudio loved her as she loved him, she didn't find it all that difficult to believe in miracles anymore.

Her pregnancy was confirmed on the eve of Flavia and King Vincente's wedding. The entire family rejoiced and were still rejoicing seven and a half months later when she gave birth to triplets, one girl and two boys. Although the babies were slightly premature and tiny, they were healthy and strong.

Their daughter was the oldest and when King Vincente laid his hand on her head and confirmed the right of progenitor, Therese almost fainted.

"I thought only males could inherit the throne."

"Where did you get that archaic idea?" Claudio asked with a laugh. "Just because Scorsolini babies are almost always male, that does not mean we do not allow our daughters to inherit. We are a modern royal family...I keep telling you that."

"But…you always talked about your nephew inheriting."

"He's the oldest."

"Oh. So, she's going to be a queen?"

"Just like her mama. Yes."

Therese grinned, exhausted from the delivery, but happier than she'd ever been. "It wouldn't have mattered. I would have loved her the same anyway."

"Of course you would…our children will know nothing but love from us all the days of their lives."

She smiled, her heart so filled with joy that some days she did not know if she could hold it all in. He'd been showing her his love in ways she could never mistake. He'd started with allowing his brothers to share more of the burden of leadership while his father was convalescing so he could oversee her return to health with minute attention.

He even stayed in the hospital with her and the tabloids had a heyday with it. Some poking fun, but most saying that it was obvious this royal family did not stick with the tradition of marrying for convenience. He had made huge inroads into spending more time together all the time and now when he traveled, she went with him.

Even when she'd been pregnant.

She reached out and took his hand, loving the feel of his long, strong fingers intertwined with hers. "I happen to know you are an expert at giving love, I have no doubts our children will know nothing but an abundance of that commodity from you."

He grinned down at her.

And King Vincente smiled at them both. "The Scorsolini men are very lucky…we must raise my grandchildren to know the blessing of love the Scorsolinis are known for."

Remembering the curse the king used to believe it was, Therese felt tears fill her eyes. "We'll make sure they know the blessing of love, Papa."

And they did…all the days of their lives.

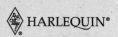

American ROMANCE®

IS PROUD TO PRESENT A
GUEST APPEARANCE BY

QUILL
BOOK
AWARD
WINNING
AUTHOR

NEW YORK TIMES bestselling author

DEBBIE MACOMBER

The Wyoming Kid

The story of an ex–rodeo cowboy,
a schoolteacher and their journey to the altar.

"Best-selling Macomber, with more than
100 romances and women's fiction titles
to her credit, sure has a way of pleasing readers."
—*Booklist* on *Between Friends*

The Wyoming Kid is available from
Harlequin American Romance in July 2006.

HARLEQUIN *Presents*

**Getting to know him in the boardroom...
and the bedroom!
A secret romance, a forbidden affair,
a thrilling attraction...**

In Love With Her Boss

What happens when two people work together
and simply can't help falling in love—
no matter how hard they try to resist?

Find out in our ongoing series of stories
set in the world of work.

On sale August '06!

HIS VERY PERSONAL ASSISTANT

by Carole Mortimer

www.eHarlequin.com

HPHVPA0806